TRUMPER

TRUMPER

HETTY BURLINGAME BEATTY

Illustrated by Joshua Tolford

1 9 6 3

HOUGHTON MIFFLIN COMPANY BOSTON

The Riverside Press Cambridge

TO SUNNYE AND JIM

TRUMPER

Trumper

1

TRUMPER DASHED down the road, the farm wagon bouncing and clattering behind him, milk cans flying in all directions. Carl hauled on the reins and yelled at him to stop, but Trumper had no such intention. With a flourishing buckjump he landed the wagon in the ditch, the harness broke, and he galloped off by himself.

Carl climbed out of the wagon muttering the worst things he could think of. The wagon was a mess and the milk cans were scattered over half a mile of road. Nothing to do but to walk the two miles back to the farm, get the big team and come back to collect the battered wagon and milk cans. Carl limped off down the road muttering angrily.

But Trumper was thoroughly pleased with himself. He had no intention of doing farm work and he hoped he'd made that clear this time. He'd been a respectable carriage and saddle horse all his life and he wasn't going to take to the soil just because Tod Sullivan had bought him for his farm! If farmer Sullivan wanted to ride cross country or drive to the village in the buggy that was one thing, but pulling noisy hayrakes and milk wagons was something else again! Trumper snorted noisily at the idea and began to enjoy the early morning gallop by himself.

The sun had just heaved itself over the sleepy hills and the air smelt good after an all night rain. Trumper tossed his head and galloped faster. It was like the early morning gallops when Bus Brown

had owned him and ridden him all over the countryside. Those were the days! Trumper felt suddenly lonely remembering Bus Brown. He slowed to a trot, then to a walk as his mood changed from unruly gaiety to loneliness. He sampled a patch of clover by the roadside, but it didn't help the loneliness and he wandered on. When he came to the logging road that led through the woods to the farm, he turned down it, heading for the barn. Perhaps any home was better than no home at all.

Halfway down the logging road Trumper remembered that he hadn't quite finished his oats when Carl hitched him to the wagon. He began to trot, thinking about the oats. By the time he reached the farm lane he was galloping again, kicking at the flapping harness as he went.

Tod Sullivan had just finished cleaning the milk room with Mark, his youngest son. As they came out of the milk room, Trumper dashed in the barn door nearly knocking them flat as he dove into his stall and buried his nose in the oats. Tod's dog, Skipper, jumped out of the way, barking furiously.

"What in glory has that horse done now!" Tod roared. "He's busted the hayrake and two sets of harness and now what in blazes has he done with Carl and the milk wagon?"

Tod Sullivan was a patient man. He loved his farm, his family, and his animals, but Trumper was too much for even Tod's patience. He stalked angrily into the stall, jerked Trumper's nose out of the oats, and said things he didn't usually say. Trumper laid back his ears and snorted, anxious to get his nose back in the oats. There was a horrid glee inside him. Maybe this time he'd made it clear that he wasn't a farm horse and didn't aim to be.

Mark took the broken harness off and hung it on a hook, while his father slipped the halter angrily over Trumper's head.

"You good-for-nothing hunk of horse," he growled. "What's got into you anyway? You never acted that way with Bus Brown, trotting around pretty as a picture and well mannered as they come! With Bus moving away I figured I had the chance of my life to get a really good horse for the light work. What the devil has come over you?"

Trumper snorted indignantly, burying his nose in the oats again. Tod came out of the stall, still furiously angry.

"We'd better harness the big team, Mark, and go look for Carl and the wagon," he said.

The team was half harnessed when Carl limped into the barn, the picture of bedraggled fury.

"Where's that blasted horse!" he stormed. "Wagon's in the ditch two miles down the road, milk cans scattered all over the country, and the milk spilled from here to there. Catch me driving that horse again!"

4

The barn crackled with anger. Mark stood between his father and his older brother, torn between being mad at Trumper and thinking he was still the most beautiful horse in the world. Even when Mark was very small he had always been thrilled when Bus Brown and Trumper had passed them on the road. Whipping along at a fast trot, his darkly dappled neck arched and his white mane flowing above it in the wind, he seemed the sort of horse a knight would ride into battle.

Two days ago, when Tod came home from the village leading Trumper behind the wagon, Mark hardly believed his eyes. He knew Trumper was for sale because Bus Brown was moving to the city, but he had no idea Tod was thinking of buying him.

"Dad!" he shouted. "Did you buy Trumper? Is he ours? Can I ride him?"

"He's ours all right!" Tod shouted back. "I just bought him from Bus. Now we've got a really first-rate horse for the light jobs!"

Mark was so excited he couldn't eat his supper. He stayed in the barn with Trumper all evening and had to be dragged back to the farmhouse when it got dark. He babbled excitedly about Trumper all the way.

"Dad, can I enter Trumper in the 4-H Club competition for the best all-round light-weight farm

5

horse? I know he'll win, and First Prize is a pure-bred Black Angus bull calf! I can start a beef herd, Dad! And if Trumper wins again next year, I'll win a heifer! You're only allowed to win twice, but I know I can with Trumper and then I'd have a bull and a heifer to start a herd! Can I enter Trumper, Dad?"

"I guess you can, Mark," Tod had said. "You should stand a good chance of winning with Trumper. Jay Strong's bay mare may give you some pretty stiff competition, though. She's handsome and she's mighty clever, and she won last year, you know."

"I'm sure Trumper can beat her, Dad!" Mark said happily.

They had walked back to the farmhouse together, making excited plans to enter Trumper in the 4-H Club competition. But the next morning Carl hitched Trumper to the hayrake to rake a patch of fresh spring alfalfa for the cows, and Trumper bolted and piled the hayrake on the stone wall, smashing it badly. They all agreed that Trumper had probably never pulled a hayrake before and got frightened by the unwieldy thing with its loud clanking noises. So this morning they hitched him to the milk wagon. Mark had teased to drive him to the station with the milk, but Carl was older and stronger and Tod said it would be better for Carl to give him a workout first, in case Trumper was still a little jumpy.

And now Trumper had wrecked the milk wagon, too, spilling a whole load of valuable milk into the bargain! Carl had always done all right with Kit and Duke, the big team of Clydesdales, but with Trumper there'd been nothing but disaster from the start. It looked as if he'd suddenly gone bad, as horses sometimes do. At least he wasn't going to be any good for farm work!

"I don't know what's got into that horse," Tod said, shaking his head in puzzlement. "Always behaved all right with Bus pulling a wagon, but we certainly can't fool around with a horse that's going to wreck all the farm equipment we hitch him to. It's hard enough to make the farm pay without major expenses like that! I can't see anything to do but sell him and get a steadier horse."

"Oh Dad, you can't sell Trumper!" Mark wailed. "I'm going to win the Black Angus bull calf with him! He'll settle down, Dad, I'm sure he will!"

"I hate to part with him, too, Mark," Tod said, "but we can't have a useless horse just standing around the barn eating his head off. Besides, you have to drive him in a hayrake and a milk wagon, as well as ride him, to win the competition, and if Carl can't do it you certainly can't. You're only twelve you know."

"Please, Dad," Mark begged, "just keep him for a little while and see if he won't settle down!"

"All right," Tod said, "but I don't know what good it will do. I don't feel like risking him with the wagon or the rake again. It costs too much to get new parts to fix them, and he might wreck them altogether. He might have hurt Carl really badly, too, you know."

"You're crazy if you keep that horse, Dad!" Carl said with feeling. "You won't catch me driving him!"

"I know," Tod said, "but it will take a little while to find another horse anyway, and if Trumper shows any real signs of settling down to farm work in the meantime, well and good. If not, we'll just have to trade him in on a horse that'll do the jobs that need doing. I'll start keeping my eye out for another horse, Carl."

Mark was heartbroken. Tod would probably buy a steady old plug and there wouldn't be a chance in the world of winning the competition!

Trumper

2

TRUMPER STOOD SULKING in his stall while Tod and Carl mended the battered wagon in the barnyard. Carl was very clever with mechanical things and he loved working on them. He liked machines better than horses, and he wished they could have a truck and a tractor to do the farm work.

Mark sat on the edge of the watering trough watching them. The wagon certainly was a mess, one axle badly bent, one shaft broken, and two of the side boards split. Carl kept muttering about Trumper as he worked, and Tod shook his head sadly as he looked at the damage.

"Lucky we didn't lose the wagon altogether!" he said. "A good wagon, too. Too bad to have it all patched up like this. Carl, you'll have to take that axle to the blacksmith and get it bent back into shape. You'd better take Kit and Duke in the big wagon and get it done this morning. We've got to have it ready to take the milk to the station tomorrow. Get back as soon as you can, so I can start plowing with the team right after dinner. Blast that Trumper horse!"

Carl harnessed the team, took the axle, and drove off to the village to get it fixed while Tod went to fix a fence in the barn pasture. Mark went on sitting on the watering trough, not offering to go with either of them. He wanted to be alone with his misery.

Finally Mark slid off the edge of the trough and wandered into the barn. He stood outside Trumper's stall, looking woefully at his handsome dappled-gray hulk in the shadowy light of the barn. Trumper turned his head and looked at him with curiosity, wondering what he was doing there. Mark went into the stall and began stroking his nose sadly.

"Why do you have to go and wreck everything?" Mark said. "I was going to win the competition with you and get a real purebred bull calf to start a beef herd, and now Dad won't let me even try you out for fear you'll wreck everything again. And he's going to sell you if you don't settle down to things quick! Please, Trumper, couldn't you behave so I can win the calf?"

Trumper loved patting and attention and he nickered softly as Mark went on stroking his nose. He didn't like Carl, but he was beginning to like Mark. Mark talked to him and petted him as Bus Brown had done, and Carl just hitched him to noisy farm stuff and tried to make him work like any old plug! Trumper snorted a bit at the idea.

Mark climbed up on the edge of the manger and spent the rest of the morning talking to Trumper and stroking his nose. He was still feeling too low in his mind to go and help his father mend the fence, and he knew that if he begged his father to let him try driving Trumper the answer would be no. The whole morning had been wasted fixing the wagon, and a load of milk lost into the bargain. If he teased his father about Trumper right now,

Tod would probably just make up his mind to sell him, and that would be that!

It was almost noon when Carl got back from the village with the mended axle. While Carl installed the axle in the milk wagon, Mark unhitched the team, watered them, led them into their stalls, and gave them their dinner. Trumper peered over the top of his stall, nickering hungrily.

"You've got to wait, Trumper, till I feed Kit and Duke. They have to plow all afternoon, and all you're doing is standing in your stall sulking because you won't work!"

Trumper snorted impatiently. At Bus Brown's he'd been the only horse and he never had to wait to be fed. He didn't like waiting while Mark fed a couple of sweaty old work horses first. Anybody ought to know enough to see he was a better horse than Kit or Duke! Finally Mark led him out to the trough for a drink and gave him his dinner. Then Mark and Carl headed for the farmhouse to get their own.

"You'd better quit moping around, Mark, and make up your mind that Dad is going to sell Trumper," Carl said. "You know as well as I do that we need an extra horse for the milk wagon and the rake, so the big team will be free for the heavy work. That was the whole idea in buying Trumper, and don't kid yourself that Dad is going to keep him after the damage he's done."

13

"I know," Mark said. "But Trumper never acted like that with Bus Brown. Seems to me he's just new around here and doesn't understand about farm work. I'm sure he can learn if we give him a chance."

"Fine idea," Carl said contemptuously, "but how many hayrakes and wagons do you think Dad is going to buy for him to practice on?"

Mark wasn't hungry. He picked at his dinner in silence and finally drank his milk and let it go at that. After dinner Tod started plowing the corn field, Carl went back to the barn to finish putting the wagon back together, and Mark went off by himself to tend his pigs.

Every spring when the big sow had her litter of little pigs, Tod gave Mark his choice of two of them to raise as his own. At the end of the summer he entered them in the 4-H Club competition for the best young pigs, and when the fair came, he sold them there. The money from the pigs was his own to keep. He had twenty-four dollars in the tin bank on his bureau, and he'd bought some things he wanted besides.

Mark's pigs were in a separate pen that his father had helped him build, next to the big pigpen. Mark went there now, seeking consolation in his misery. At least he had the pigs to show at the 4-H Club, and he'd won several prizes on ones he'd raised before. This year one of the pigs looked particularly promising, an extra big one, well built and handsomely marked black and white. Mark leaned over the fence and the pigs came grunting up to him, begging to be scratched behind their itchy ears.

"Good boys," Mark said. "You just keep on growing and maybe I'll win something at the Club show anyway."

It was poor consolation and the idea didn't cheer Mark up much, but it was better than nothing. He got the shovel and the hose and cleaned the pen until it positively shone. Tod believed that clean pigs grew better and were healthier than dirty ones, and he'd built the pens with concrete floors that could be hosed down and kept really clean. The other farmers laughed at Tod and his pampered pigs, but they had to admit that Tod got better prices for his than they did!

When Mark finished cleaning the pen, he got a brush and scrubbed the pigs themselves, rinsing them with the hose. The pigs loved the scratchy feeling of the brush and stood still, grunting contentedly while Mark scrubbed them. When he got through they really were handsome. Mark went out and cut them an armful of fresh alfalfa and watched while they ate it hungrily. Then Carl turned up with Skipper following him.

"Now that you're in a pig-cleaning mood, how about helping me clean out the big pen?" he said.

"I finally got the wagon fixed and there isn't enough time left to start a big job."

"OK," Mark said, and carried the shovel and the hose over to the big pen. When they opened the gate, Skipper dashed in, barking furiously at the big sow and her litter of babies. He took a dim

view of pigs and felt they needed heckling at every opportunity. The big sow grunted angrily and the small pigs squealed and yelled with terror, trying to hide behind their mother. The big sow held her ground for a few minutes, then charged Skipper with loud grunts and murder in her eye. Skipper beat a hasty retreat, jumping the fence for safety. Mark and Carl howled with laughter as

Skipper sat down sedately at a safe distance. It was the first time Mark had laughed all day and it felt good.

When the pen was clean, Mark called Skipper and set off for the upper pasture to bring the cows in for milking. It was a long walk up the lane and the steep hill to the pasture, and Mark dawdled along looking at things along the way, while Skipper chased rabbits in the fields. He stopped to talk to the chipmunk that lived in the wall by the lane, but in his gloom over Trumper he'd forgotten the crust of bread he always brought her. The chipmunk popped out of her hole and ran along the wall to Mark.

"Sorry, Chippy," Mark said. "I forgot all about your bread crust today!" Chippy sat on her hind legs, then ran up Mark's arm and sat on his shoulder, scolding and nibbling his ear indignantly. Mark reached up and stroked her soft back.

"I really am sorry, Chippy," he said. "I was just too busy thinking about something awful and I forgot your bread. Dad is probably going to sell Trumper and I just couldn't think about anything else!"

Chippy chattered angrily, then jumped down to the wall and scampered back into her hole, still scolding. Mark went on up the lane, feeling badly that he'd let his friend down.

At the foot of the long hill Tod had built a stone

pool around the spring and stocked it with fish to keep mosquitoes from breeding in the water. No one was allowed to catch these fish, and they'd grown fat and lazy. Mark usually brought bread for them, too, but not today. It was hardly worth stopping, with no bread to feed them, so Mark went on up the hill to the pasture and got the cows. Skipper rounded them up neatly and Mark trudged along behind them back to the barn.

While Tod and Carl did the milking, Mark watered and fed the horses and forked fresh bedding into their stalls. When the milking was finished, Tod and Carl set the big milk cans in the milk room trough to cool, and Mark turned the cows out in the barn pasture for the night. With the chores finished, they all headed back to the house for supper.

Mark still wasn't hungry. After supper he read a farm magazine, but his thoughts kept wandering back to Trumper. Saturday night and no lessons to do, so he went to bed early and lay tossing and turning until he heard Carl coming up to bed. He was in no mood to talk to Carl. He knew he'd get no sympathy from him about Trumper, so he turned his face toward the wall and pretended he was asleep.

Trumper

3

SUNDAY was a day of rest for men and horses both, nothing to do but milk the cows morning and night and feed the animals. After the morning milking, Mark and Skipper took the cows to the upper pasture for the day and fiddled along on the way back. The rest of the family had gone to church in the wagon with Kit, leaving Mark to tend farm till they got back. Mark had remembered to bring some bread crusts this time, and he fed the fish and Chippy before going back to the barn to see Trumper.

Trumper was feeling lonely and neglected and he nickered when he heard Mark coming. Mark went into his stall, sat on the manger, and stroked Trumper's nose, but there didn't seem much to say and he just sat there silently, feeling very low in his mind. He wished it had been his Sunday to go to church because he liked the singing and he

19

thought maybe it would help to say a prayer about Trumper. Finally he decided to say one anyway, so he sat on the manger and said, "God, please make Trumper behave so Dad won't sell him and I can win the bull calf, Amen."

He felt it wasn't much of a prayer, but maybe it was better than nothing. He heard the wagon coming and then Carl came in leading Kit to her stall. "You still sulking over that Trumper horse?" he asked unfeelingly.

"You would too, if you liked Trumper and wanted to win a bull calf to start a beef herd," Mark said crossly.

"Well, how about feeding the horses while I unharness Kit? It's almost dinner time, and you've got to quit sulking sometime you know! It isn't as if sulking would change things," Carl said with a horrid air of elderly wisdom.

Mark knew he was right, much as he hated to admit it. He slid down off the manger and went to work.

After Sunday dinner, Tod stretched out on the porch hammock to read his paper, while Carl worked on a radio set he was making out of mail order parts. Kathy, the youngest, went off to the shed to play with her pet rabbits. Mark helped his mother wash up the dinner dishes before going back to the barn to see Trumper again.

It was a beautiful spring day and the barn

seemed dark and stuffy, coming into it out of the bright May sunshine. "Want me to take you out for a walk, Trumper?" Mark asked.

Trumper nickered happily, glad of company. Mark unfastened the hitching rope and led him out

into the lane, letting him stop to munch the fresh green clumps of clover along the way. Trumper kept nickering happily, glad to be out stretching his legs a bit in the spring sun. He was good and sick of standing all day in his dark, stuffy stall!

When they came to the path that led to the creek Mark turned down it, Trumper following him doc-ily enough. At the edge of the creek, Mark tied Trumper to a tree and went swimming. The water was still cold, but it felt good and Mark splashed around for a bit, tried a few dives from the flat rock, then climbed out to dry himself in the sun. He sat on the rock that hung out over the creek and watched the fat bass that lurked under it. He usually spent Sunday afternoon fishing, but he'd forgotten his fishing pole. His mind was too much on Trumper. But Trumper was happily eating grass and didn't seem to have a care in the world.

"You know, Trumper," Mark said, "Carl is right. Sulking isn't going to fix anything for you or for me either. We've got to figure this out! You've got to learn to do farm work and I've got to figure some way to teach you without Dad knowing. He won't let me try if he knows."

Trumper nickered and moved closer to Mark, nuzzling him with his nose. He thought Mark still sounded sad and worried and he wanted to comfort him.

"It's all very fine your nickering and making up to me," Mark said, stroking Trumper's nose, "but it would make a lot more sense if you'd settle down and do some work around here without wrecking everything! Then you could stay, and I could win the bull calf and start a beef herd!"

Trumper nickered and nuzzled some more, but Mark ignored him. It was time to go after the cows, and Mark untied the rope and led Trumper back to the barn. When they got to the barn door, Trumper hung back, nickering sadly and looking longingly at the green sunny hills.

"Want me to lead you with me when I go for the cows? I guess that wouldn't hurt anything and it would give you some exercise," Mark said.

Then suddenly Mark had a better idea!

An old saddle and bridle had hung on a sawhorse in the feed room ever since Mark could remember. He'd often climbed up on the saddle, pretending he was riding a real horse after cattle on the open range. Tying Trumper to the water trough, Mark went to the feed room and hauled the saddle out of its dusty corner.

Maybe it was a foolish idea to try to ride Trumper, but Bus Brown had always ridden him without any trouble. Maybe Trumper was just afraid of noisy hayrakes and milk wagons because he wasn't used to them. Mark dragged the heavy saddle out to the trough and laid it down in front of Trumper while he went back to get the bridle and saddle blanket. When he came back, Trumper was sniffing the saddle, nickering happily.

"You want me to ride you?" Mark asked doubtfully.

Trumper tossed his head and nickered gaily. Mark was still doubtful, but Trumper stood very still while Mark put on the saddle blanket and hoisted the heavy saddle onto his back. Then he slipped the halter off and reached up to put the bridle on. Trumper put his head down so Mark

could reach, and opened his mouth for the bit. Mark began to laugh. It really did look as if Trumper was in favor of this project.

When the bridle was on, Mark climbed up on the trough and from there into the saddle. Excitement crowded out fear as he took up the reins and said, "Giddap." Trumper walked off down the lane, tossing his head.

The barn was hidden from the house by a long row of trees and no one saw Mark riding down the lane on Trumper. Mark was glad of that. He knew he'd be told to get off that crazy horse at once, before he got his neck broken! Both his father and Carl had given up thinking anything could be done with Trumper, and they certainly wouldn't have figured he was a safe horse for Mark to ride!

But Trumper had different ideas about it all. At last someone had waked up to the fact that he was a good saddle horse and not a farm plug! It was like the days when Bus Brown had ridden him, and he danced with happiness as he went down the lane.

"Good boy," Mark said softly. "Even if you'll just help me bring the cows in maybe Dad will let you stay! That's a little something useful anyway."

Trumper whiffled a happy whiffle through his nose as they started up the long hill to the pasture. Chippy and the fish were forgotten as Mark headed for the pasture gate and slid out of the saddle to open it. He had to climb on the fence to get back in the saddle. Trumper was a big horse and his back was a long way from the ground, but he sidled close to the fence and stood still so Mark could get on.

The cows were at the far end of the pasture, close to the swamp where the grass was greenest. They looked up in surprise when they saw Mark on horseback instead of on foot. Skipper, who was dozing on the farmhouse porch waiting for Mark to call him, wasn't there. The cows stared foolishly, as cows do, and walked off into the swamp. Without Skipper to chase them out, they thought they had it made!

"Come on, Trumper," Mark said, nudging him with his heels. "We've got to get them out of there and back to the barn."

Trumper sploshed into the swamp, Mark guiding him skillfully in rounding them up. In a few minutes the cows gave up and headed lazily toward the pasture gate, with Mark and Trumper at their heels. Trumper had never herded cows before, but he decided it was fun to make these big clumsy creatures go where Mark wanted them to. He took to the job with real enthusiasm.

"Good boy!" Mark said again, stroking Trumper's handsome neck. "I bet you can learn to work on a farm if they give you half a chance!"

Trumper

4

CARL AND HIS FATHER were standing by the barn door waiting for the cows. Skipper was standing beside them, his ears pricked up, listening and looking toward the lane.

"Funny Mark didn't take Skipper with him to get the cows," Tod said. "He always calls him when it's time to go. You don't suppose that boy has forgotten all about the cows, do you? He's in such a sulk over that Trumper horse he's liable to forget anything."

"No telling what he'll do these days!" Carl said. "I told him to quit sulking but I haven't seen him all afternoon."

Carl glanced into the barn. "Dad! Trumper is gone! He isn't in his stall."

"*Now* what?" Tod said in exasperation. "I suppose he broke his rope and just took off. I wouldn't put it past him!"

They were just going to examine the rope in Trumper's stall when the cows turned into the barn lane. Behind them was Mark on Trumper, Trumper dancing and tossing his head as he followed the cows. Tod's first thought was for his son's safety.

"What in glory are you doing on that crazy horse!" he said as softly as he could, afraid of startling the unruly Trumper if he shouted.

"Trumper's all right, Dad," Mark said gaily. "He hasn't done a thing wrong, even let me get off at the gate and get back on again. He likes being ridden! He just doesn't like old rattly hayrakes and milk wagons behind him."

Tod pushed his milking cap back and scratched his head as the cows trailed past him into the barn and Mark pulled Trumper to a stop outside the door.

"Just maybe you're right at that!" Tod said. "I never really thought of that because Bus had him so well trained to pull a buggy. Maybe if you ride him after the cows right along he'll settle down and get used to things around a farm."

Tod patted Trumper's neck, and Trumper nickered and leaned toward him for more patting, but as soon as Carl came closer he reached out and nipped at him indignantly. Carl jumped back out of Trumper's reach.

"He doesn't like me." Carl grunted angrily.
"And that goes for both of us! I don't like him either, not even a little bit! I'd take a truck or a
tractor over a horse any day, but if we can't have

those I'll stick to old Kit and Duke. At least *they*
don't wreck everything!"

Tod gave Carl a pained look. Carl certainly had
no way with animals! But he was very clever with
machinery, mighty good at repairing the farm
equipment, and a good worker, too. Tod put his
hand on Carl's shoulder.

"Cheer up, son," he said. "I can't say I blame you for not liking Trumper after the things he's done to you. If he doesn't settle down soon, I'll trade him in on a steadier horse. Just give Mark a chance with him first."

"That's all very fine," Carl said, "but don't forget that haying is coming up next month and that's when we need an extra horse the most, a steady, hard-working one that isn't full of crazy notions!"

"I know," Tod said. "Tell you what. If Trumper hasn't settled down before haying time I'll sell him. That gives Mark almost a month to work it out in. If he hasn't succeeded by then, Trumper goes. That's a promise, Carl!"

Mark said nothing. He was torn between desperate hope and fear of failure. At least his Dad was giving him a chance, even if it wasn't a very long one. He slid out of the saddle and led Trumper into his stall.

"You heard what Dad said," he said softly. "If you settle down fast and get to work, you can stay. If you don't, you have to go. Please, Trumper, be good the way you were today, and learn to pull the wagon and the hayrake besides! Then you can stay! Dad said so."

"Time to get to work," Tod called from his milking stool. "No fair taking time out from your chores for Trumper. You'll have to do that in your free time!"

30

"OK, Dad!" Mark shouted back.

He unsaddled Trumper quickly, fed and watered all the horses, and bedded them down for the night with clean straw. His heart was shouting inside him as he worked. Maybe there was time after all. Maybe Trumper would learn quickly. At least he could be ridden, and that was a start.

But Trumper was thinking other thoughts in his stall. He'd been promoted to his proper place as saddle horse, and he meant to keep it that way! He didn't know that Mark was aiming to turn him into a farm horse.

At supper that night, Mark could hardly keep his mind on his food he was so busy trying to think of ways to teach Trumper to work.

"Look, Mark," Tod said, "if you're going to give up eating altogether for thinking about Trumper, you'll be too weak to handle a kitten, much less an unruly horse!"

Mark bolted his supper with sudden speed and gulped down his milk without coming up for air. After supper he did his lessons as fast as he could, trying terribly hard to keep his mind on them.

The next morning he was up before the sun and off to the barn to saddle Trumper. The cows were in the barn pasture for the night, as usual, so there was no need to ride after them. Trumper was wide awake and raring to go as soon as Mark got the saddle off its peg. Mark put it on as fast as he could,

31

put on the bridle, backed Trumper out of his stall, and led him to the trough so he could climb on.

In a minute they were off down the lane, Trumper sniffing the early morning air and snorting a little with excitement. Mark headed him up the hill past the upper pasture and along the trail that led to the big forest beyond it.

It was dark inside the forest, the pale light of dawn filtering dimly through the immense trees. Mark could just make out the trail and he guided Trumper along it. It was an old, old trail, first made by the Indians, and it hadn't changed since. The giant trees on either side were bigger than they had been, and the logs laid down to make a bridge across the swampy spots were moss grown and rotting with age. But they were still passable, and Mark and Trumper slid through the trees like shadows, the sound of Trumper's hooves deadened by the thick leaf mold.

A red fox trotted across the trail in front of them, stopping in surprise to look at them before disappearing again among the trees. A few minutes later, two deer ran across the trail, startling Mark and Trumper both. It was a bit scary in the dark, lonely forest at that time of day.

But Trumper was loving it. This was really like the old days with Bus Brown. He longed to go faster, go for a real top speed gallop as he had with

Bus, but Mark hadn't urged him on yet so he just walked faster, waiting for Mark to give him the signal.

After half an hour of fast walking through the forest, they came out on the ridge that rolled down into the next valley. The sun was just coming over the hills on the far side, turning the valley golden, its farms and fields looking small and far away at the bottom. A dog barked, and Mark saw that a farmer was herding his cows in for milking at the farm below them.

"Oh gosh, Trumper." Mark said suddenly. "It must be milking time! Dad will kill us both if we're late."

He wheeled Trumper around and headed for home. The forest was lighter now and the trail smooth and soft before them. "Come on, Trumper, we've got to hurry! Let's gallop!"

Mark leaned forward in the saddle and touched Trumper's sides with his heels. That was all Trumper was waiting for. He leaped forward in a fast, smooth gallop, with Mark hanging on for dear life and loving it. Together they raced through the forest, the now wide awake birds and animals, rushing away before them.

It only took them ten minutes to cross the forest at a gallop. They came out above the pasture, panting and happy and Mark slowed Trumper for the steep hill down to the farm. At the bottom they raced along the lane again and came thundering up to the barn door.

Startled by the sound of Trumper's galloping hooves, Tod came out to see if Mark was all right.

He saw Mark sitting gaily in the saddle, his face red with the wind and excitement.

"You're late, Mark," Tod said. "You remember I told you not to let Trumper interfere with your chores."

"I know, Dad," Mark said unhappily. "We went

through the forest and it took longer than I thought. We galloped all the way home, trying not to be late!"

"You might as well leave Trumper saddled while you feed the team, so you can take the cows to the upper pasture after milking. You can feed him when you get back. Better to let him cool off a bit first."

"Yes, Dad!" Mark said, his spirits soaring again. He'd been afraid his father would be really angry about his being late and maybe not let him ride Trumper any more.

Mark worked harder than ever the rest of the day to make up. He really tried to do well at school and did some extra chores when he got home. Tod smiled at him, knowingly, realizing he was trying to make up.

Trumper

5

ALL THE NEXT WEEK Mark rode Trumper in every free moment. He went on getting up early in the morning for a gallop around the countryside, but he was careful not to be late again for his chores. He began teaching Trumper to mind his voice, without using the reins or nudging him with his heels. He thought it might help in teaching him to do farm work. By the end of the week, Trumper was getting quite good at it.

But this still wasn't teaching Trumper to pull milk wagons and hayrakes. A whole week was gone and there were only three weeks left before haying! Mark wracked his brains trying to think of a way to teach Trumper to pull rattly things behind him, without risking either the wagon or the rake. He searched the wagon shed, hoping there might be some old wreck he could experiment with, but everything there was useful and in good condition. Then his eye fell on an old stone sledge that was rugged and battered. It looked like the

best bet, hard to damage and too heavy to run away with easily.

Sunday afternoon, with plenty of time to spend on it, Mark sneaked off to the barn by himself. He took Trumper's well-patched work harness off the hook and dragged it into the stall. Trumper, who had been nickering a welcome to Mark, gave one look at the work harness and laid back his ears defiantly.

"Trumper," Mark said sternly, "behave yourself! You've got to learn to work and right now is when we start!"

Trumper hung his head and looked pathetic, but his ears were still back and he was snorting little snorts. Mark didn't like the look of it much, but he went ahead and put the harness on anyway. Trumper went on sulking and snorting, but at least he didn't kick or plunge. When the harness was on, Mark backed him out of the stall and led him to the wagon shed.

The stone sledge was just inside the open front at one end of the shed, and Mark led him up to it and turned him so he could hitch him on. Trumper turned his head and saw what Mark was doing. He let out a terrifying snort and started to walk off. Mark hauled on the reins and stopped him, but he refused to back up to the sledge. Mark struggled with him for half an hour without making any headway. It looked hopeless and Mark was close to tears. He sat down on the sledge to think and Trumper stood watching him with a happy glint of victory in his eye.

"It's not funny, Trumper, and you're not so smart! Who ever heard of a horse that wouldn't work? You're just plain stubborn and lazy, that's what you are!" Mark's voice was halfway between anger and tears.

Trumper pricked up his ears, then walked over to Mark and nuzzled him with his nose, but Mark refused to pat him and went on sitting on the sledge, lost in thought. Finally an idea popped. He got up, led Trumper over to the trough, and climbed onto his back on top of the work harness.

"Get going!" Mark said crossly, and Trumper walked off down the lane without protest, the work tugs dragging in the dirt.

"No farm can keep a horse that's only good for riding, Trumper! Can't you see that Dad will sell you sure as shooting if you don't learn to work? PLEASE, Trumper!"

Mark rode him up and down the lane a few times, then back to the wagon shed. Trumper gave one look at the sledge and refused to go near it. One of the choked-up sobs in Mark's throat came out. Trumper heard it and looked around inquiringly.

"All right — go ahead and get yourself sold! Keep me from winning the bull calf. Be a stupid, pigheaded mule if that's the way you want it!" Tears of hopelessness were running down Mark's face in spite of himself.

Trumper nickered in an effort to comfort him, but Mark couldn't choke back the sobs of bitter disappointment. Trumper stood still for a few minutes, not knowing what to do to comfort Mark, then slowly he walked over to the sledge and stood in front of it.

Mark didn't believe it, but as Trumper went on standing there, nickering softly, he decided he'd give it one more try. He slid to the ground and hitched the tugs to the sledge. Trumper just stood there, hanging his head and looking as pathetic and long suffering as he possibly could.

Mark took up the reins and said "Giddap," his voice still tearful and hopeless. Trumper walked forward at a snail's pace and the sledge slid along the dirt behind him.

"Good boy!" Mark said encouragingly, still not believing Trumper meant to buckle down to it.

But Trumper did! He went down the lane, putting one foot slowly ahead of the other, head hanging, his ears flopping sideways at a completely woebegone angle. He looked so completely ridiculous that Mark began to laugh. Trumper stopped and looked back at him with a look of profound pathos and reproach. He looked so sad that Mark went and stroked his nose.

"Good fellow!" Mark said softly. "Just stay with it and we'll work things out yet."

Trumper felt comforted by Mark's more cheerful voice and affectionate petting. When Mark said "Giddap" again, he went on pulling the sledge, still looking pathetic and still moving slowly, as if his last moment had come. But he kept going, at least, and new hope bounced up in Mark's heart.

At the end of an hour, Mark put the sledge back in the shed and led Trumper back to the barn, where he took off the work harness and put on the saddle. Trumper came to life the minute he saw the saddle. His head went up, his ears forward, his neck arched with a proud look. He whiffled happily through his nose.

Mark laughed until he couldn't stand up and had to go and sit on the edge of the water trough. All the pent-up hopelessness and sudden relief of the afternoon came out in laughter, rocking him back and forth.

"Oh Trumper," he gasped, "you are the foolishest horse that ever lived!"

He climbed into the saddle, still gasping from laughing so hard, and they went for a gallop, bringing the cows in on the way home. Tod and Carl had no idea that Mark hadn't just been riding all afternoon, and they greeted him casually when he led Trumper into the barn. Mark was dying to tell them about Trumper pulling the sledge, but he was just a little afraid that the sledge might be one of Tod's treasures, although it didn't look like much. If Tod told him not to use it, there'd be no way to train Trumper, so Mark kept it secret.

The week dragged by endlessly. With school and chores afterward and getting the cows back and forth, there was only time for short rides on Trumper. Time was running out and Mark was more and more worried. He was afraid that his father and Carl wouldn't think just pulling the sledge was enough to make them change their minds about Trumper's uselessness. Haying would start in a little over two weeks, and they had to have a steady horse for the milk wagon and the rake by then. Mark's heart sank as the days went by without time to teach Trumper more.

The next Sunday, Mark hitched Trumper to the sledge again. Trumper rebelled at first, but gave in sooner this time, and hauled the sledge up and down the lane, still looking extremely sorry for himself. After several trips up and down the lane, Mark tied Trumper to the water trough and went into the milk room. There were four big empty milk cans standing in the corner, and Mark dragged them outside, one by one, and loaded them on the sledge. Trumper watched him suspiciously while he tied them on with a rope.

"Now, Trumper," Mark said, "this is where you learn to haul milk cans! And please don't dash off and bust them or kick them to bits when they rattle. Dad will kill me if you smash those good milk cans!"

Mark untied Trumper, took up the reins, and shouted to him to go ahead. Trumper started off at a walk and the cans set up a horrible rattling.

Trumper quivered all over, laid back his ears, and got ready to plunge.

"Trumper, don't!" Mark shouted desperately.

Trumper stopped in mid-plunge and stood still, his ears back, his head tossing nervously. Mark went to his head and stroked his nose.

"Those milk cans aren't going to jump off that sledge and bite you, Trumper. Now behave yourself and pull them down the lane without smashing them. You just have to!"

Mark took Trumper by the bridle and led him, and Trumper followed, still tossing his head and threatening to take off. The cans rattled and banged together on the sledge making a horrible noise, but with Mark at his head, Trumper pulled them down the lane with no disaster. Mark led him till he quieted down, then took the reins and drove him from behind. All went well this time. Up and down the lane they went for an hour, then Mark put the cans back in the milk room, and took Trumper for a gallop as a reward.

"If you'll only keep on from here, Trumper, and get steadier about it, we can show Dad next week how good you are. Maybe he'll see how much you've learned and let you stay! Trouble is he's going to need you for the rake and the wagon in two weeks. What are we going to do about that?"

Trumper nickered softly. He felt he'd done mighty well and he knew that Mark was pleased with him. He didn't like the idea of doing farm work any better than he had to start with, but Mark was so awfully unhappy when he didn't cooperate in it! Trumper nickered again and then sighed. Why wasn't Mark content just to ride him and let it go at that. It was so much more fun!

Trumper

6

"ONLY TWO WEEKS till haying, Mark," Carl said at breakfast the next morning. "I suppose you'll have Trumper all trained and ready to work by then! Dad, how long are you going to let Mark fool around with that horse? We can all see he's all right for riding, but what we need is a work horse."

"I know, Carl," Tod said. "We'll have to do something about it soon. It isn't fair to Duke and Kit to put all the work on them, and it slows the haying badly. We've lost quite a bit of hay other years because of that, the rain spoiling the cut hay before we could get it in. Next weekend I'll see if I can sell Trumper and find a better horse. I'm sorry, Mark, but it's just got to be done!"

Mark's heart sank into his shoes with a thud. He wasn't going to have two more weeks to teach Trumper in.

"But, Dad, he's learned so much!" Mark wailed. "I didn't tell you because I was afraid you'd be cross, but Trumper's been pulling the stone sledge all right! I even put some empty milk cans on it, and he finally settled down to that, too!"

"You shouldn't have taken the milk cans, Mark, without asking me," Tod said, scowling. "You know that, Mark. I would have helped you if you'd asked me, but even so it will take weeks of practice to settle him down enough to trust him with the wagon and the rake. You can't do these things in a minute! You heard me promise Carl that we'd have a steady horse by haying time. I've got to keep that promise, Mark!"

Mark left the table and ran all the way to the barn, fighting back the tears. He dashed into Trumper's stall, threw his arms around his neck and sobbed as if his heart would break.

"They're really going to sell you, Trumper!" he sobbed. "Next weekend! Dad is going to get another horse, and all because you won't settle down and work. I tried to tell you, Trumper! And just when you were learning, too."

Mark broke down altogether and wept a deluge of hot, hurting tears into Trumper's white mane. Trumper nickered in distress and nuzzled him gently, overcome by Mark's grief. He didn't know what it was all about, but he knew something was terribly wrong. He had grown to love Mark even

46

more than he had loved Bus Brown, and now Mark was sobbing his heart out!

In a little while Tod and Carl came in to do the milking. Mark tried to stifle his sobs, but a choking splutter came from Trumper's stall. Carl said nothing and went to get the cows in from the barn pasture, but Tod came into the stall and put his arm around Mark's heaving shoulders.

"I'm really sorry, Mark," he said. "I know how much you think of that horse and how much you want to keep him and win the competition and the bull calf with him. But this is a farm, Mark, and we all have to work to keep things going. You and I and Carl all work hard, and your mother does, and Kit and Duke do. That's the way life is. You can't make a go of things if you don't work for them! The trouble with Trumper is he wants everything for free, his feed and all the care you take of him, and a dry barn to live in. You have to earn these things, and he only wants to do what he likes to do. That's the trouble."

"I know, Dad," Mark sobbed, "but if we only had a little more time. He's learning, Dad. He really is!"

"Mark, I promised Carl. It isn't fair to him to make the work so hard for lack of an extra horse. Besides, I'll really try to find a good one, one that you can win the competition with. I honestly will."

47

"But, Dad, I love Trumper! And he loves me," Mark wailed.

"I've said I'm sorry, Mark. That's all I can do. We have to start haying just as soon as school lets out, and there's no way around that. You do your chores, Mark, or you'll be late for school." Tod's voice was kind but it was firm.

Mark came out of the stall silently, his face red and swollen, and started watering and feeding the horses while Tod and Carl started the milking. Mark knew his father was right about the farm and about working, but he felt so certain that Trumper was right on the edge of settling down to work, and he was sure no other horse could be as wonderful as Trumper. As he did his chores, Mark was thinking desperately of some way to save Trumper. It had to be right off! There were only five days left before Tod would lead him away and sell him. Mark hatched a really desperate idea.

It was Mark's job to harness Kit or Duke to the milk wagon while Tod and Carl loaded it with the heavy cans. This morning he was slow about leading the horse out. Tod and Carl both knew how badly he felt about Trumper so they didn't hurry him. Carl turned the cows out in the barn pasture for Mark to drive up the hill on Trumper. No one noticed that Mark had put Trumper's work harness on instead of Kit's.

Suddenly Mark ran out of the stall to the pasture

door as if he heard something. He looked out, then shouted to Tod and Carl, who had just finished loading the milk wagon. "Dad! Carl!" he shouted. "The white heifer is having her calf down by the fence and she's having trouble!"

Tod and Carl didn't stop to think. They knew the calf was due and no farmer takes a chance of losing a good heifer for lack of help at calving time. They ran out the pasture door and started down the hill toward the heifer.

Mark dashed back into Trumper's stall. He was sobbing again, with real desperation this time. "Trumper, this is it! It's your only chance!" he sobbed, backing Trumper quickly out of his stall.

Trumper sensed that this was really desperate. Mark wanted him to do something, and wanted it desperately this time. He was still sad because he knew Mark was terribly unhappy over something. He longed to comfort him somehow and make things right again. The only way he could think of was to do what Mark said.

Mark led him quickly out to the loaded wagon and backed him so suddenly between the shafts that Trumper didn't have time to protest. In a minute he was hitched on and Mark jumped into the seat and took up the reins.

"Now!" Mark sobbed from the seat. "Get going, Trumper, and don't wreck anything or spill the milk!"

Mark's voice sounded so desperate that Trumper obeyed without stopping to think. As he lurched forward, the milk cans clattered loudly behind him. He quivered all over, half started to

plunge, then remembered Mark's sobbing desperate voice, and settled down to the load. He trotted down the lane at a good clip, going steadily, evenly, and fast.

Tod and Carl looked up from the pasture and saw them go.

"Mark!" Tod shouted at the top of his lungs. "Come back with that wagon this minute! If that horse wrecks it and spills the milk I'll whip you both till you can't stand up! Come back!"

Mark had never seen his father so angry before. He began sobbing harder than ever, but he didn't come back.

"Keep going, Trumper," he sobbed. "We've just got to get this milk safely to the station. If you don't Dad will kill us both for sure!"

Trumper settled down to a faster trot. He thought he knew now what Mark wanted of him and how much it meant to him. They went down the road at a good clip, boy and horse together, both with only one thought in mind—to get the milk safely to the station.

An hour later they trotted back down the lane, yesterday's empty milk cans rattling loudly in the wagon. Tod was cultivating the cornfield by the lane. He stopped the team and shouted at Mark.

"Where's the milk?"

"At the station." Mark shouted back. "These are yesterday's cans, same as always."

Tod's anger, which had been boiling to a peak in the last hour, was battling with his pride in his son, a boy that would risk everything for the horse he loved. Not only risk it, but win! No one but Mark could have got that horse to do that job and do it safely. Somehow he'd got Trumper to do it.

Tod didn't know how. He only knew that there was a bond of devotion between the boy and horse that could work miracles, miracles even a dumb beast could understand. Tod was so overcome he couldn't say anything. He didn't trust himself to speak. He started up the team and went on down the cornfield in silence.

Mark was frightened by his father's silence. It must mean that he was too furiously angry to speak. After all, Mark had not only risked the wagon and the load of milk, which he had been absolutely forbidden to do, but he had lied to his father about the heifer in order to do it! Besides that he was very late for school.

Mark drove Trumper to the barn, unhitched him, and led him into his stall. The cows were gone from the barn pasture, and Mark realized that Carl must have had to take them to the upper pasture before he went to school. Mark was overcome at the number of things he'd done horribly wrong in order to prove to his father that Trumper could be trusted with the wagon. In his desperation to save Trumper from being sold, he hadn't stopped to think what the consequences might be. Maybe his father would sell Trumper anyway as punishment.

Mark took Trumper's harness off in a daze of anxiety and remorse. He couldn't bring himself to go to school so late and have to face the teacher with the story of what he had done. Besides, Carl would be at school and Mark didn't dare face Carl either! He went back into Trumper's stall and stayed there, stroking his nose and silky neck.

"Oh Trumper," he said softly, "you were such a good horse to pull the wagon safely. You did everything just right and I did everything all wrong. I don't know what Dad will do."

Trumper nickered affectionately, puzzled over what was wrong now. He'd pulled the wagon

safely to the station but Mark was still terribly upset over something. Trumper couldn't understand, but he nuzzled Mark fondly, trying to comfort him.

Mark stayed in Trumper's stall the rest of the morning not knowing where to go or what to do. It was almost noon when he heard his father bringing the big team in from the cornfield. Mark stood very still, hoping Tod wouldn't know he was there, trying in panic to postpone the terrible moment of facing his father's anger.

Tod led Kit and Duke into their stalls, slipped off their bridles and put on their halters, leaving the rest of the harness on for the afternoon's work. Then he came over to Trumper's stall and looked in.

"Mark, come out here," he said in a strained, tense voice.

Mark came out and stood before him, his face white, his eyes full of tears he was trying to hold back.

"What you did this morning was terribly, terribly wrong, Mark," Tod said quietly. "You shouldn't have risked the wagon and the load of milk, and you shouldn't have lied to me about the heifer in order to do it. I never knew you to do anything so wrong!"

"I know, Dad," Mark said in a shaking voice. "But Dad, you were going to sell Trumper without giving him another chance! I only wanted to show you he'd really learned to do better. You wouldn't let me try him in the wagon when I asked you. I knew Trumper could do it if he had a chance!"

"Well, he did do it," Tod said. "I'll have to admit that. I was probably wrong, not letting you try it at least, but that doesn't make what you did right! But you have done well with that horse, and you deserve credit for that. I'll tell you what I'll do, Mark. If you think Trumper will do it, you can go on taking the milk to the station, but the first milk he spills will be the last. One more smashup and he goes, and no more argument about it! And you'll have to start early enough to take the cows up and get to school on time, too. Is that clearly understood?"

"Yes, Dad, it is!" Mark said, overcome with relief and gratitude to his father. "I know Trumper can do it, Dad, I just know he can!"

"All right, son," Tod said. "But don't forget the conditions!"

"I won't, Dad!" Mark promised, and he dived back into Trumper's stall.

"Oh Trumper!" he gasped. "You did it and you will go on doing it, won't you? You heard what Dad said, you can stay if you'll go on working and behaving yourself."

Trumper nickered happily at the sound of relief in Mark's voice. Whatever the terrible thing was that had made Mark so unhappy, it seemed better now! Trumper nickered again and nuzzled Mark's face.

Trumper

7

THE NEXT MORNING Mark was in the barn before daylight. He watered and fed the horses, harnessed Kit and Duke so they'd be ready for Tod, then put on Trumper's work harness. Trumper was disappointed at not being saddled for an early morning ride instead, but there was an intenseness in Mark's voice that made him realize there was still a crisis afoot.

Mark talked to him as he put on the harness, a combination of happy, excited chatter and tense pleading.

"You've got to keep on, Trumper! If you let down now, Dad will sell you and there won't be another chance this time. You did so wonderfully yesterday. Just keep it up and you can stay, and I'll bet I can win the calf, too!"

Mark let the cows in from the barn pasture and

had them in the stanchions when Tod and Carl came to do the milking.

"Quite a lot of sudden efficiency this morning," Carl said sarcastically. He was feeling a bit sore at his father's letting Mark off as easily as he had yesterday. "Don't forget you haven't got it made yet. I'll bet that Trumper horse hasn't any idea of settling down for keeps!"

"That'll do, Carl," Tod said. "Mark understands the terms: he can go on keeping Trumper as long as Trumper behaves, not one day more. Don't keep rubbing it in, Carl. Give him a chance."

"OK," Carl said a little bitterly, "but I bet you wouldn't have let me off that easily if I'd done anything that bad!"

"That's hardly fair, Carl," Tod said. "You never did anything that bad, so you don't know what I'd do if you did, and you've got to remember how hard Mark has worked at teaching that horse."

Carl said nothing and buckled down to milking. When milking was finished, he and his father loaded the milk wagon, and Mark led Trumper out to hitch him on. Mark had spent the milking time pleading softly with Trumper in the stall. Trumper was torn between thorough resentment of this milk-wagon thing being repeated and the effort to do what Mark wanted him to. He looked a bit skittish as Mark led him to the wagon and, for a moment, it looked as if he were going to refuse to back up between the shafts.

"Please, Trumper!" Mark said with his heart in his voice. "Please! You've *got* to."

Trumper backed up, reluctantly, and Mark hitched him to the wagon and climbed into the seat. Tod and Carl stood watching, anxiety in both their faces. It wasn't a very safe project for a boy Mark's age to drive a horse like Trumper. Tod was really alarmed when he saw how skittish Trumper looked with his head held tensely high and his ears back. But Tod had promised his son a chance, and he kept quiet.

"That horse will kill Mark yet." Carl muttered.

"Easy, Trumper, easy, boy." Mark said softly. "Steady! You did it yesterday and you can do it today! Now get going, and take it easy."

Trumper stepped forward and started down the lane at a walk. By the time he reached the end of the lane, he was trotting at a good clip. Carl and his father watched them out of sight, both wondering if Mark would make it again in one piece.

Out on the road, Mark was still talking to Trumper, steadying him with his voice, half pleading, half praising. Trumper gradually relaxed his skittishness and settled down to a fast trot, the milk wagon rattling along steadily behind him.

When they got back to the barn almost an hour later, Tod and Carl were still puttering around the barn. Neither of them had said much, but they were both worried about Mark and couldn't put their minds on much else till they saw him safely back. They looked up as Mark drove up to the barn door, but neither of them said anything, trying to conceal how worried they had been.

Mark unhitched Trumper and led him into the barn.

"Dad?" he said. "Can I ride Trumper up to the pasture with the cows, and then ride right to school from there? I can tie him in the buggy shed at school and ride him home after. It would save a lot of time and, besides, it would be a reward for Trumper every day after pulling the milk wagon."

"Sounds sensible enough," Tod said, "and it would give you a little more time to work with Trumper, without cutting into other jobs."

Carl gave a disgusted snort. "So now Mark gets to ride to school while I walk."

"You can ride Trumper to school any day you like." Mark grinned, with a look of pure deviltry in his eye.

"Heck, no!" Carl said hastily, and went off to get his school books.

Mark took off Trumper's work harness and put on the saddle. Trumper brightened immediately, dancing with happiness. They rounded up the cows, herded them to the upper pasture, then galloped to the schoolhouse, Mark's lesson books bang-ing against the saddle. Mark had taken them to the barn with him, to be sure not to be late for school again.

Trumper waited patiently in the buggy shed while Mark was in school. There were two other horses in the shed, both of them belonging to boys

who lived too far from school to walk. One of the horses was a very old farm horse, too old to work and looking pretty bony and moth-eaten. He was an amiable old character and carried the three sons of his owner to school on his broad flat back, all three sitting bareback in a row. Trumper looked at the shoddy old fellow and gave a snort of contempt. The other horse was very small, too small to work, and was a mottled dun color. The farmer who owned him had bought him cheap, because of his small size and lack of style, as a means of getting his only son back and forth to school. At least he had a saddle on and Trumper nickered and made friends with him at once. The old horse was dozing anyway, and didn't seem to mind Trumper's contempt for him.

After school, Mark galloped home on Trumper, did his other chores, and then rode Trumper after the cows. It had been a long, exciting day, and Mark could hardly keep awake to do his lessons that evening. As soon as he finished them he went to bed and was asleep before his head touched the pillow.

The rest of the week went well. As soon as Trumper found that he had the gallop to school with Mark to look forward to after hauling the milk wagon, he began to take a better view of things. Pulling the wagon wasn't really so bad, once he got used to it, and by the end of the week he was making no protest at all.

At breakfast Saturday morning Tod said suddenly, "Mark, when you get back from taking the milk to the station, how about driving the whole family to town in the wagon with Trumper? We need some groceries and supplies, and Trumper seems to have settled down pretty steadily the last few days. Kit and Duke have been working hard and we can turn them out to pasture for the weekend."

"OK, Dad!" Mark said enthusiastically. "Will do!"

It was always fun in the village on Saturday and the whole family looked forward to it. Carl had

taken the cows to the upper pasture while Mark took the milk, so Mark drove Trumper to the farmhouse on the way back from the station and the whole family piled in. Mark and his mother and father sat on the seat, and Carl and Kathy climbed in the back where the milk cans usually went. When Trumper saw Carl approaching the wagon, he laid back his ears and looked around to be sure Carl wasn't going to do the driving. He relaxed when he saw Mark take up the reins. As Trumper got started along the road to the village, he suddenly realized that this was no farm-horse job but a family jaunt to town, a real carriage-horse job! His head went up, his neck arched, and his ears pricked forward as he swung into a spanking trot, just as in the days when Bus Brown had driven him in the buggy.

They whipped up Main Street at a fast clip, a proper cloud of dust rolling out behind the wagon. Kit and Duke were good faithful horses, but they were plodders and certainly lacked zip and style as carriage horses. Trumper had plenty of both, and everyone on Main Street stopped to watch the arrival of the Sullivans that morning. Quite a crowd gathered at the hitching rail while Mark tied Trumper.

"How come the boy can handle that horse?" one of the farmers asked. "I heard you couldn't use him at all and wanted to sell him!"

"Mark has a way with him," Tod said proudly. "He's got him pulling the milk wagon to the station every morning, steady as can be. But he won't do a thing for the rest of us!"

There was a murmur of surprise and admiration

63

as everyone looked at Mark. Mark stroked Trumper's nose fondly.

"He's a good horse!" Mark said. "Just needed a little time to get used to farm jobs. I guess he never did any before."

Tod went to the feed store, while his wife went to buy groceries with little Kathy tagging along after her. Carl made a beeline for the radio shop to see what was new, and Mark headed for the harness shop. It was his favorite place in the village, with its good smell of new leather and rows of shiny harness and bits hanging along the walls. In the middle of the shop there was a life-size wooden horse for displaying extra fancy harness. The horse was painted dappled gray, like Trumper, and it always wore the finest harness in the shop. Sometimes it wore the latest thing in buggy harnesses, but today it wore a beautiful set of light work harness with a red, padded collar and sparkling brass knobs on the tops of the hames.

Mark walked slowly around it, admiring the shining buckles and softly polished leather. He thought of Trumper's well-worn, badly patched, and battered harness, and he wished with all his heart that he could get a harness like that for him. He already had twenty-four dollars saved, and maybe if he saved all his pig money this year he'd be able to. It would be wonderful to have a harness like that for the 4-H Club competition!

When all the errands were done and the wagon loaded with calf feed, tools, and groceries, Tod suggested an ice-cream soda. They all trailed off thirstily to celebrate.

Trumper

8

Monday morning dawned hot and sunny, perfect haying weather. School was over at last and Mark and Carl felt liberated with plenty of swimming and fishing ahead. No more lessons to do, and haying was fun even if it was hard work.

Tod hitched the big team to the mower and set off for the north meadow, while Mark took the milk to the station and the cows to the pasture with Trumper. Carl dragged the hayrake out of the wagon shed to give it a good overhauling and finish repairing the damage Trumper had done to it a month ago.

When Mark got back, he put Trumper in his stall and went out to help Carl. Carl looked up a bit grimly from his work.

"There's probably not much use fixing this rake if you're going to hitch Trumper to it tomorrow," he said. "I suppose Dad is going to let you try that, *too.*"

"I don't know," Mark said soberly.

Mark didn't want to discuss the hayrake project with Carl or anybody else. He was too worried

about it himself. Trumper had finally settled down reluctantly to pulling the milk wagon, but the hayrake was a big, clumsy, noisy thing that almost any self-respecting horse might thoroughly object to! But the hayrake was part of the agreement with Tod, and it was also part of the 4-H Club competition. Trumper had to pull it, or else.

By Tuesday morning the hay Tod had cut the

day before was dry and ready to rake. The sun was still beating down hotly on the hayfield, but black thunderheads were piling up along the horizon.

"We've got to get that hay in fast," Tod said at breakfast. "It looks like a heavy rain before night. Mark, if you think Trumper will pull the rake, Carl and I can load the hay on the wagon and haul it to the loft while you rake. We don't want that good hay spoiled in the rain!"

"I'll try Trumper, Dad," Mark said, trying to sound confident about it.

"There goes the rake again," Carl snorted. "I just finished fixing it yesterday, Dad, and now you're going to let Trumper wreck it again!"

"That's the best hay on the farm," Tod said, "and if it gets rained on now it will be half mouldy all winter. Give Mark a chance with Trumper, anyway. If Trumper won't do it, we'll just have to leave the hay where it is. No use raking it with Kit if we can't get it in the loft before the rain, and we need both Kit and Duke on the wagon. There won't be time to rake first and load afterward. Trumper is the only chance of getting it in time!"

"He'll do it Dad!" Mark said a little desperately.

"All right," Tod said. "Carl, you take the milk to the station with Duke, while Mark gets Trumper on the rake and starts raking. We can leave the cows in the barn pasture to save time."

Mark harnessed Duke to the milk wagon, while

Tod and Carl hurried with the milking. Then he put on Trumper's work harness, talking as he worked. Trumper thought it was for the usual milk-wagon job and couldn't understand the new anxiety in Mark's voice.

"This is going to be different, Trumper," Mark said softly. "You've *got* to pull the rake so we can save the hay. And please, Trumper don't wreck the rake again!"

Carl drove off in the milk wagon, and Mark led Trumper out to the hayrake, which Carl had left standing in the barnyard, ready for use.

"Can I help you, son?" Tod asked, his voice sounding worried.

"I don't think so, Dad," Mark answered. "I'll just have to talk to Trumper about it myself."

Tod smiled, but he went on standing by the barn door, ready to help if Trumper got too unruly. He knew that if anybody could get Trumper to pull a rake, Mark could, but he was worried about Mark's safety just the same.

Trumper had the hangdog look he reserved for pulling milk wagons, but when he saw the rake he planted his feet and refused to move. Mark tried to pull him toward it, but Trumper kept backing away instead.

"You've just got to help, Trumper, whether you want to or not!" Mark said pleadingly. "If you don't, the hay will be spoiled and Dad will sell you and everything will be awful."

Trumper stood with his feet planted, torn between doing what Mark wanted him to and determination not to go one step further in becoming a farm horse. He'd finally given in about the milk wagon, just to please Mark, but a hayrake was something else again! He eyed the rake with profound contempt and snorted.

"Please, Trumper! You've *got* to!"

The desperation in Mark's voice was plain enough and Trumper wanted terribly to please him. Slowly and reluctantly he walked toward the rake.

"Good boy!" Mark said happily. "I knew you'd do it. Now back up so I can hitch you on."

Trumper backed gingerly between the shafts, his ears laid back, his lips curled with distaste. He stood still while Mark fastened the tugs, his ears still laid back and a look of resentment in his eye.

"Now look, Trumper," Mark said severely, "if you wreck the rake this time, you're through!"

Trumper nickered meekly and hung his head while Mark climbed onto the seat and took up the reins. Trumper stood still with his head hanging down, the picture of abject misery and self-pity.

"Oh come on!" Mark said impatiently. "Quit sulking and get going. You've got to get that hay in whether you like it or not. Get going!"

Trumper started walking down the lane, the rake clattering loudly behind him. His ears were still back and he lifted his head and began tossing it in a tense sort of way that Mark didn't like the look of!

"*Please,* Trumper, don't smash the rake, and me too."

There was real fear in Mark's voice now and Trumper heard it. He stopped in his tracks, turned

his head, and looked at Mark sitting on the rake behind him. He realized he was scaring Mark badly and he was ashamed. He must stop scaring him somehow!

"*Please,* Trumper!" Mark said again, his voice torn between fear and pleading.

Trumper nickered softly and walked off toward the hayfield, trying to look as safe and reliable as he possibly could.

Tod watched them out of sight from the barn door, smiling with pride and amusement. "No accounting for the way that horse lets that boy handle him," he said to himself.

"Where's Mark?" Carl asked, as he drove the milk wagon up to the barn.

"Raking with Trumper," Tod said.

"That horse will kill Mark!" Carl exclaimed. "Don't let him do it, Dad! It's crazy!"

"Instead of standing talking," Tod said, "let's get the team hitched to the hay wagon and get out there so we can keep an eye on them."

As the hay wagon turned into the meadow, they saw Trumper and the rake standing very still at the edge of the unraked hay. Mark was sitting on the seat looking very angry.

"Get going, mule!" he shouted at Trumper.

Trumper hung his head. He didn't like the way Mark said that word. Trumper had no idea what a mule was, but it didn't sound like a good thing to be.

"Mule. Good-for-nothing mule!" Mark said even more angrily. "Get going!"

Trumper gave a deep sigh and gave up. Slowly and deliberately he started down the field. Mark stepped on the lever of the rake, dumped the hay, and dropped the rake back into raking position with a loud clatter. Trumper lifted his head with a start and walked faster.

"That's more like it!" Mark said. "Just *keep* going now. We'll never get this hay in if *you* don't. If farming is good enough for me it's good enough for you, too!"

Trumper buckled down to it, figuring that if he couldn't get out of it, he might as well get it over as quickly as possible.

"Good boy!" Mark said, as Trumper turned at the wall for another swathe of hay, the windrows getting straighter and neater as they went.

"Well I'll *be*," Carl said, as he and Tod followed with the wagon, loading the hay on board as they went. "I don't know what Mark does to that horse, but he surely seems to have him licked!"

"Just has a way with him, I guess," Tod said, stopping for a minute to mop the sweat off his face.

At the end of three hours of steady work the raking was finished and Mark drove over to the wagon. Tod patted Trumper's sweat soaked neck affectionately. Trumper whiffled happily and reached out for more patting and praise.

"Better unhitch him from the rake, Mark, and tie him to the back of the wagon while we finish this load. You can drive the team for us, while Carl and I load. That'll make it quicker."

Mark took Trumper out of the rake and tied him to the wagon where he could reach the new, sweet hay.

"Good, good boy!" Mark said happily. "You did

it. You really did it! Maybe now we can save the hay."

Mark climbed on the wagon and started the team. The long morning wore on, the sun beating down on the hayfield with the stifling heat that comes before a storm. The clouds piled higher and blacker on the horizon and thunder growled in the distance.

By noon the new load was ready to haul to the loft and Tod shouted to Mark to drive the team in by himself. It was the first time Mark had been allowed to drive the loaded wagon in. It took both strength and skill to guide the powerful team down the narrow lane and through the loft door with a full load. Tod and Carl rode on the wagon, resting their tired backs and mopping the sweat from their faces and necks.

"I couldn't have done that better myself," Tod said, as Mark pulled the team to a stop in the loft. "I guess you're a full-fledged farmer now, Mark."

Mark was bursting with excitement. He'd been trusted with a man's job and had done it successfully, and Trumper had raked the hay! Mark slid down off the wagon and untied Trumper to lead him to his stall.

"Better just give the horses hay, and water them after they cool off," Tod said. "We can't risk foundering them in this heat. They can have a good feed of grain tonight when the work is finished."

Carl unhitched the big team while Mark led Trumper down to his stall and gave him a loving hug. Trumper nickered happily and stuck his nose into the manger looking for more hay. He was hungry after the hard morning's work, and Mark went to fork it down for all three tired, hungry horses. He was tired and hungry himself, but he whistled as he worked.

Trumper

9

Mark's mother had a quick lunch ready for them, piles of big sandwiches and jugs of hot coffee and cold milk. She knew it was a race against time to get the hay in before the storm and there'd be no time to eat a hot dinner. Time enough for that when the hay was in.

Tod and the boys bolted the sandwiches as fast as they could and went back to the barn. Trumper's work was finished for the day, but the big team still had a hard afternoon's work ahead of them hauling the rest of the hay to the loft and unloading it with the hay fork. Mark watered the thirsty horses and hitched the team to the wagon and they all rode out to the field.

All afternoon they worked in the heavy heat, Mark driving the team and Tod and Carl forking and loading as fast as they could, while the black clouds piled higher and higher in the sky, finally covering the sun. The thunder was growing into an angry roar. By three o'clock Tod said they wouldn't

lose much now even if the storm broke, and by four the last load was on the wagon. Mark headed the team for the barn. A cool wind whipped across the hayfield, bringing the first big drops of rain with it.

A fork of lightning darted across the sky like a snake's tongue, followed by a crackling roar of thunder.

Just as Mark turned the team into the barnyard, the storm broke with the fury it had been slowly piling up all day. The rain sluiced down, soaking them to the skin in a minute, and the wind hit the wagon broadside, threatening to blow it over. A brilliant flash of lightning followed by a crash of thunder threw sober Kit and Duke into sudden panic, and they plunged toward the steep bank that went down to the lower level of the barn and the safety of their stalls. Tod grabbed the reins from Mark and pulled the team back into the lane and through the loft door. It took all his strength to hold the frightened horses.

In a minute they were inside the loft and out of the deluge of rain. Only the top layer of hay was wet, and Carl forked it off on the floor to be dried later. The rest of the load was dry and Tod said to leave it on the wagon till morning. The rain was coming down too hard to hitch the team to the un-loading fork. They unhitched the tired horses from the wagon and let them rest and munch hay in the loft while the storm raged outside.

"No need to hurry now," Tod said. "The job's done and we just made it. Thanks to Mark and Trumper we didn't lose even a wisp of hay! Without them we'd have lost half of it, *at least*."

They stretched out on the soft, good-smelling hay, resting their tired muscles and listening to the wild rain pounding on the roof, the roar of the wind in the trees, and the crash of thunder that followed every lightning flash. It was good to rest after the hard day's work, and the storm had brought cool air after the stifling heat. They talked and laughed while the storm thundered away outside. Mark's heart was singing inside him. Trumper had saved the hay! He wouldn't be sold now!

In half an hour the worst of the storm was over. As Mark led Kit and Duke down to their stalls from the loft, a rainbow stretched across the sky and Mark felt it was a good omen for Trumper.

The cows, out in the barn pasture during the storm, were glad to come in out of the wet. As soon as the door was opened they crowded in, all twenty of them trying to get in first, their black and white hides clean and shiny with rain.

Tod and Carl settled down to the milking while Mark tended the horses. He led them out to the trough for a drink, then gave them an extra big feed of oats and plenty of hay. They had well earned a good feed that day. While they were munching happily, Mark cleaned their stalls, put down fresh bedding, then got the curry comb and brush and cleaned their sweat-matted coats.

He brushed Trumper until he glistened, talking to him as he brushed.

"You did it, boy! You did it!" he kept saying. "Now you can stay here, and as soon as haying is over we'll start practicing for the competition. We'll win that bull calf yet!"

Trumper nickered happily, his nose still buried in the oats.

The next morning the sun rose into a cloudless sky and the whole world sparkled after the rain. All that week and the next, the sun shone day after day, and haying went on steadily and well. Trumper made a few more objections to the hayrake, but finally settled down to it. He was slowly beginning to understand that it was a proud thing to do a job well and be trusted with it. All along he had felt superior to old Kit and Duke. He felt he was too good to do the sweaty jobs they did, but he realized finally that they had had Tod's affection and respect from the start and he had only won it when he did his work as they did.

After the haying was finished, there was a long stretch ahead for other jobs before harvesting the oats and corn, and time for Mark and Carl to go swimming in the creek between jobs. This was the time of year they loved best.

There was still plenty of work to be done, fences and walls to be repaired, new roofing to put on part of the barn, and a new pump to install in the milk room. Mark was old enough to be a real help now. It wasn't quite as much fun as driving the horses, but it was an important part of farming and Mark liked it. It was good to see a sagging fence come straight and strong again, or a leaky stretch of roof made tight and dry against the weather. It made Mark feel like a real farmer, able to turn his hand to anything, and he and Carl and their father talked and laughed together as they worked.

Mark was still taking the milk to the station every morning with Trumper. He began practicing for the competition in real earnest now, teaching Trumper to do quick turns with the wagon, back up to the milk platform at the station with a real flourish, and walk, trot, or stop at a spoken command.

"You've got quite a horse there!" Dave at the milk station said one morning, when Mark and Trumper did an extra-fancy backing job at the platform.

"I'm training him for the 4-H Club competition in October," Mark said proudly. "Do you think he'll win?"

"Looks as if he stands a good chance to," Dave said. "Of course Jay Strong's mare is mighty clever, too. Won last year, you know."

"I know she did," Mark said. "But me and Trumper have just got to win it this time! Mr. Hubbard is giving a Black Angus calf from his champion herd for the prize, and I'm aiming to start a beef herd."

"Well I sure hope you win, Mark. You've earned it—all the work you've put in training that horse. He sure was a hellion at the start!"

Mark drove off happily. Even Dave had noticed what a good horse Trumper was.

As soon as Mark got back from taking the milk, he saddled Trumper and took the cows to the upper pasture. Herding on horseback was another event in the competition and Mark used the cows to practice on. The poor cows had never worked so hard before on their way to the pasture, but Tod said it was all right as long as Mark didn't run them. Trumper learned to stop them in the lane, holding them rounded up in a tight bunch. He learned to turn them this way and that, herd them against a fence and hold them there, or drive them in a straight line, all at a single word of command from Mark. They practiced every day and Trumper loved it. Herding was his favorite sport!

Whenever Mark had enough time off, he hitched Trumper to the rake and practiced with that. Trumper took a dim view of the rake still, but Mark was determined and Trumper finally settled down to really trying. Mark had to practice this one himself, because perfect timing in lifting and lowering the rake was essential to making neat straight windrows. He had to practice with imaginary hay, as the fields were bare since haying, but he finally got

a rhythm into the thing that seemed as if it ought
to work.

The end of August, Mark took his two pigs to the
4-H Club Pig Show and won a Second Prize on the
larger one. Bill Smith had a better pig and won
First. Mark was disappointed because he wanted
extra good pigs this year for a special reason, but

the big pig was certainly good, and the smaller one
wasn't half bad. Mark hoped he'd get a good price
for them at the Fair. When the Fair came to the
next town, Labor Day weekend, Mark hitched
Trumper to the wagon, loaded the pigs on board,
and he and Tod set off to sell them. Tod always
went along to the Fair to see what was doing in the
farming world.

They watched the cattle judging, both milk and

beef cattle, saw the horse show, and took a look at the pigs, chickens, and geese. Tod was especially interested in the geese.

"I think I'll get some goslings next spring," he said. "They can wander around the farm and swim in the creek, and they'd taste mighty good roasted!"

When the pig sale came up, Mark took his pigs into the enclosure with about a hundred others. His pigs were fat and sleek and clean as could be. The big pig brought thirty-five dollars and the smaller one twenty-three. Mark was delighted and folded the money away carefully in his pocket.

"What you going to buy with it?" Tod asked curiously.

"That's a secret," Mark said. "I'll show it to you when I get it. I wish school wasn't starting tomorrow! I'll have to wait all the way until Saturday to get it."

They drove home and Mark put the money in his tin bank before he did his chores.

Trumper

10

ALL THE NEXT WEEK was wrapped up in starting school again. Mark would have enjoyed it more if he hadn't been so impatient for Saturday to come so he could carry out his secret project. He went back on his old schedule of taking the milk to the station and the cows to the upper pasture with Trumper, then riding to school. There was no time on weekdays for practice in herding now. The cows were undoubtedly relieved at being allowed to go peacefully to the pasture without the fancy herding operations along the way, but Mark and Trumper both missed it.

Saturday finally came, and Mark asked if he could ride Trumper to the village as soon as his chores were done.

"I guess so," Tod said. "I have to haul some heavy stuff this week, so the rest of us can go in the big wagon with the team."

Mark hurried through the chores that morning, then dashed off to the village at a dead gallop on Trumper. They charged up to the hitching rail in front of the harness shop, and Mark slid out of the saddle, tied Trumper, and bolted into the shop, his heart in his mouth. As soon as he got inside he gave a yip of relief. It was still there!

Mark walked round and round the big wooden horse in the center of the shop again, looking at the beautiful work harness on it. This time he felt the leather, touched the shiny buckles, and reached up to touch the solid brass of the hames with their glistening knobs.

Old Mr. MacGregor, who ran the shop, came over to help Mark admire it. "Quite a harness, eh Mark?"

"It's beautiful!" Mark said softly. "How much is it, Mr. MacGregor?" Mark held his breath while he waited for the answer.

"Well now, let's see. I'll have to look it up in the catalogue. Your Dad thinking of buying it?"

"No," Mark said excitedly. "I'm thinking of buying it myself, but I don't know if I have enough money. I have eighty-three dollars. I don't suppose that's enough for such a good one!"

"Well, I dunno," Mr. MacGregor said, thumbing through the well-worn catalogue. "I think it's around in there somewhere. It's more than a regular harness, 'course, because it's such a fancy one, good quality, too. The best leather there is. Ah, here it is. Eighty-seven dollars and fifty cents, and worth every penny of it!"

"Oh," Mark said, his heart sinking with a thud. "I haven't got quite enough. Oh, gosh!"

Mr. MacGregor looked at Mark's stricken face. "I can give you a good harness for less, just not so fancy, but good, stout quality just the same."

"It was this one I wanted specially, Mr. Mac-

Gregor! I wanted it for Trumper to wear in the 4-H Club competition. His old harness is all busted and mended and looks terrible! You see, I want to win the Black Angus bull calf Mr. Hubbard is giving for a prize. Then I can start a beef herd."

"Hmmm," Mr. MacGregor said, scratching his chin. "D'you say you've got eighty-three dollars? That's mighty close. I guess I can let you have it for that for the competition, although I won't be making much on it. I took off ten percent for cash already. But you take it, Mark, for eighty-three!"

"Gee, Mr. MacGregor!" Mark yipped. "That's wonderful of you! But couldn't you just keep it for me till I can earn the extra four-fifty? It would take a little while. With school and chores and all, I won't be getting much chance for outside jobs but I'll sure try hard if you'll just hold it for me."

"Why don't you try it on Trumper and see if it fits, lad? If it fits, it's yours for eighty-three dollars. Your Dad has been a mighty good customer of mine for a lot of years, and I'd sure like to see you win that competition!"

"Gosh! That's wonderful, Mr. MacGregor! Could we try it on him now? He's right outside."

"Sure, sure. Help me take it off of here, and we'll put it on him right now."

Mark started unfastening the beautiful buckles as fast as he could, holding his breath with excitement. Suppose it wouldn't fit after all! He hadn't thought of that, but the wooden horse looked almost Trumper's size and the harness was a little loose on it.

"There's room for adjustment on all the straps, y'know," Mr. MacGregor said, seeing Mark's excitement and suspense. "They don't skimp any on these good harnesses."

When the harness was off they carried it out to the hitching rail. It looked even more beautiful out in the sun, the brass knobs and buckles flashing in the bright light. Mark slid Trumper's saddle off quickly, and they began putting the harness on. Mr. MacGregor started with the collar and hames.

"That's the important part," he said, as he lifted the collar around Trumper's neck and fastened the buckle. "If a collar doesn't fit, you get sore shoulders for sure, and we wouldn't want those on a handsome horse like Trumper, would we now?"

Mark watched him as he examined the collar with skilled eye and fingers. Mr. MacGregor wasn't one to hurry, and Mark nearly burst holding his breath while he waited for the verdict.

"Hmmm," Mr. MacGregor said, putting his head on one side to squint at the collar, "look's to me as if it was made for him!"

"Golly!" Mark shouted. "Does it really! Do you think the rest will fit?"

Mark slipped Trumper's riding bridle off quickly and put the new bridle on, while Mr. MacGregor put the rest of the harness on with a slowness that was maddening. The bridle fitted by letting it out a hole. Mark stood back and looked at its shining bit and the bright brass studs around the headband. Trumper lifted his head proudly, tossing it so the sun glistened on the bright brass and the gleaming nickel of the bit.

"Golleee!" Mark exclaimed, popping with excitement. "Does that ever look beautiful on him! Does the rest of it fit, Mr. MacGregor?"

"It sure does," the old man said with a pleased grin. "You know that harness on that handsome horse is sure going to be a good ad for my shop. Wouldn't be surprised if I'll have to order some more of those when people see that one going around on Trumper!"

They both stood there, lost in admiration as Trumper danced a little, setting all the brass to sparkling. Trumper was well aware of the admiration and nearly bursting with pride and excitement himself.

"Funny how a horse always gets all set on himself in a new harness," Mr. MacGregor said. "Just like a woman with a new dress! Vain critters, I guess."

Mark put his hand in his pocket, pulled out the eighty-three dollars, and gave it to Mr. MacGregor. Just then Kit and Duke came ambling up the street with the big wagon and all the family on board.

"Hey! Dad, Mom, Carl! Look at Trumper!" Mark shouted.

"Well, I'll *be*," Tod said, getting out of the wagon and coming to look. "So *that's* what you did with your pig money. That's the big secret, eh! You're going to have Trumper looking like a show horse in that rig."

"I hope he doesn't bust *that* one," Carl said, with his usual distrust of Trumper's behavior.

They all got out of the wagon and gathered around to admire, and everyone on Main Street joined the crowd. Trumper arched his neck and went on tossing his head, basking in the praise and admiration.

"Dad, could you haul the saddle and bridle home in the wagon?" Mark asked. "I'll ride Trumper home bareback with the harness on. I can't wait to see how he'll go in it."

"Sure thing," Tod said, grinning. *"That* boy," he said to the gathered crowd, "nothing is too good for that horse of his! Next thing you know, he'll have that horse in Hollywood instead of working on a farm. That boy!"

Everyone laughed, caught up in Mark's excitement and really impressed by the beautiful harness on the handsome Trumper. Mark thanked Mr. MacGregor gratefully for the bargain, climbed up on the hitching rail, and from there to Trumper's back. He hooked up the tugs so they wouldn't drag in the dirt, and he and Trumper went down the street at a proud trot, headed for home.

The next morning, Mark drove the family to church in the wagon with Trumper and his new harness. The congregation stood outside admiring it so long that they were almost late getting into their pews. Trumper stood in the carriage shed, looking proudly down his nose at all the other horses.

Tod started harvesting the oats the next day, with Kit and Duke pulling the heavy harvester. It was a good crop this year and the weather was dry and sunny all that week. As soon as Mark and Carl got home from school in the afternoons they helped load the golden sheaves of grain and haul them to the barn for threshing, stacking them outside the barn where the threshing machine would stand. Mark's only regret this year was that the oats didn't need raking. The harvester did the whole job, cutting the grain stalks close to the ground, sliding it along the moving platform, and tying it in neat bundles that fell out behind as the big machine moved along behind the team.

Tod harvested every morning, and when the boys got home from school they hitched Kit and Duke to the hay wagon, Tod and Carl loading the grain while Mark drove the team. On Thursday the threshing machine came early in the morning, pulled by the old chuffing steam engine that ran it.

Some of the larger farms had their own threshing machines with modern gasoline engines, but the smaller farms still hired Big Joe and his old steam engine to go from farm to farm to do the threshing.

Mark heard the engine whistle down the road and ran down the lane to meet it. He climbed aboard, greeting Big Joe enthusiastically, and they clanked and chuffed up the lane, yelling bits of news to each other above the noise. Mark told Big Joe all about Trumper, and his hope of winning the competition and the bull calf.

"I've heerd tell about that horse," Big Joe shouted. "All the farms down the line are a' talking about him. They was tellin' me how he wrecked everythin' he was hitched onto till you took him over. Is that right? They say he's steady's a lamb now!"

"That's right!" Mark shouted back happily, as the noisy engine rolled into place in front of the loft door.

"Quite a kid, ain't you, to handle a horse like that?"

"Trumper's quite a horse!" Mark shouted happily.

They pulled the thresher into position and fastened the long belt that ran it from the steam engine. The engine belched black smoke, sounding as if it were going to either fall apart or blow up, and the thresher started pouring grain into the grain bins and golden straw into the loft. It took two days to thresh it all.

"Dandy crop this year, Tod," Big Joe commented when the job was finished and the big engine throttled down to a weary panting noise.

"Not half bad at all!" Tod said happily. "If we always get as good as that, we'll surely have nothing to complain about."

"Hope you do!" Big Joe shouted, as he throttled up the engine again and started it crawling off down the lane, headed for the next farm.

Trumper

11

Big Joe came back two weeks later when the corn was harvested, towing the corn chopper and blower behind his black, smoky engine. Tod and Carl forked the long stalks of corn into the chopper, and the chopper fed it in small pieces into the long pipe, like a smokestack, that led to the little door at the top of the silo. Forced air blew the chopped corn up the pipe and into the silo. Big Joe let Mark run the steam engine, which chuffed and blew out clouds of black smoke as it turned the wheels of the machinery. The silo was filled to the brim when they finished, plenty of good cow feed for the long winter ahead.

September slipped into October and the day of the 4-H Club competition finally came. Mark was beginning to think it never would, but it did. He had spent every free moment practicing with

Trumper, but after school started there wasn't much time for it. Mark hoped desperately that Trumper hadn't forgotten anything he'd learned.

October twelfth was the big day and the sun came up in a golden ball, turning the autumn leaves into a mass of brilliant color. Carl took the milk to

the station with Kit that morning, giving Mark time to give Trumper a final brushing and the harness an extra polishing. As soon as Carl got back, Mark hitched Trumper to the milk wagon, put the saddle and bridle in the back, and drove off to the competition grounds. The rest of the family followed in the big wagon. It was a real holiday picnic, an all-day do with hot dogs and ice cream at noon and the whole family was looking forward to it.

Mr. Hubbard, who was sponsoring the competition and giving the Black Angus calf for First Prize, owned the biggest farm in the community and his Black Angus herd was famous all over the country. He was all wrapped up in beef cattle and horses, and he put on this competition at his own expense to encourage beef raising and better horsemanship among 4-H Club kids.

Horses, wagons, and cars were already collecting from all over the countryside when Mark and Trumper arrived at the big field used for the competition. The second-growth hay had been mowed the day before for the raking competition, and a herd of fifteen Black Angus cows were milling around in a pen, waiting for the herding. A wagon height platform, like a milk station platform, had been built near the judging stand, with a complicated course laid out in flags around it. Anyone whose horse or wagon knocked down a flag would be disqualified, and Mark's heart sank when he saw how narrow the distance between the flags was. It seemed only a few inches wider than a wagon!

The bull calf, a nine-month-old weaner, was in a pen by itself beside the judging stand, its sleek, black hide glistening in the sun. Mark thought he had never seen such a beautiful animal. He drove past it into the field and pulled Trumper to a stop in the area reserved for the contestants. His heart was pounding with excitement and anxiety as he looked around at the five competitors already there. There was a white horse he didn't know that looked promising, but the others didn't look too good. Most of them he knew, and he shouted a greeting to their drivers.

Then Jay Strong's bay mare arrived, with young Peter Strong driving her. She came into the field at a fast trot, her red coat shining, her black tail and mane combed and brushed till they looked like silk. Mark knew that this was the horse he had to fear most. She was not only handsome, but her dark eyes and well-shaped head spelled intelligence as well. She handled beautifully as Peter swung her around and pulled her to a stop beside the other wagons.

"Hi, everybody!" Peter shouted gaily, looking altogether too self-confident for anyone's comfort.

"Hi," Mark said anxiously.

"So that's the Trumper horse I've been hearing about," Peter said. "He's handsome all right! I remember when Bus Brown had him, but I heard you had a lot of trouble making him do farm work! Looks aren't everything in this show, you know. Cleverness is the main thing, knowing how to do the jobs cleverly and well. That's what you win on."

"I know," Mark said halfheartedly.

Trumper nickered politely to the handsome mare beside him, tossing his head and arching his neck as well as he could. But Mark wasn't half as enthusiastic about the pretty mare as Trumper was. He knew that right there stood the main chance of not winning the bull calf!

Two more contestants drove in, making a total of nine. Mark knew them both and shouted a greeting. One of the horses had good action and handled mighty well, and Mark thought to himself he'd have to look out for that one, too.

The roadside was packed with wagons and cars now, and people were swarming around the edge of the field. In a few minutes Mr. Hubbard got up in the judges stand and shouted that the competition was about to begin.

"Clear the field, please!" he shouted. "The first event will be the milk-wagon contest! Each wagon will be loaded with eight milk cans filled with water. If any contestant spills a can he's out. And if any horse or wagon knocks down a flag, he's out. Joe James will put numbers on the contestants, and they'll compete in order, starting with number one. There are men at each section of the course to give directions to the contestants. Let's begin! Number one horse onto the course, please."

The gray horse at the end of the line stepped forward at an easy walk, Bill Peters driving him. He went to the start of the course, got directions from the man standing there, and started down the course at a good trot. At the end of the straightaway he had to turn and back a hundred yards to the platform. The gray went beautifully on the straightaway, and he started to back well. But after fifty yards of backing he got rattled and impatient, and got the wagon crooked. Bill had to drive him forward a few paces to straighten the wagon and clear the flags. Again the horse backed well for a few paces, then really got out of hand and knocked down a flag!

"Number One disqualified!" Mr. Hubbard shouted from the judging stand. "Let's see what Number Two can do!"

The next horse moved forward, a moth-eaten looking black driven by Dick Joels. The horse certainly didn't look like much, but he went through the course with a quiet patience and deliberation that gave him a perfect score. There was no speed or zing to his performance, but he certainly knew what he was doing and Dick handled him beautifully.

The next horse knocked down a flag right at the start, by getting excited and out-of-hand on the easy straightaway. The next three horses made a perfect score although two of them had to be stopped and started again on the backing in order to keep going straight.

Jay Strong's bay mare, Number Seven, was next.

She trotted gaily over to the starting line and went through the course fast and perfectly, Peter handling her with real skill. A shout of applause went up from the watching crowd. Mark's heart

sank. He was next in line, and he didn't see how Trumper could outdo a performance like that.

"Number Eight, please!" Mr. Hubbard shouted from the stand.

"Come on, Trumper!" Mark said softly. "Easy now, don't rush it. And for gosh sakes be careful!"

Trumper tossed his head and moved forward at an easy trot. A murmur of admiration went up from the crowd as he swung into the course, neck arched, ears forward, his beautiful gray hide and silver mane shining in the sun. At the end of the straight-away, Mark turned him and started backing just as he had practiced over and over again at the milk station.

"Easy now, Trumper, easy! Don't rush it," he kept saying softly.

Trumper did it perfectly, and an enthusiastic cheer went up from the crowd.

The last horse flubbed it altogether and was disqualified. That left six horses still in the competition.

"Hayraking next!" Mr. Hubbard shouted. "Unhitch your horses from the wagons and use the rake standing over by the hay. Each contestant will rake three swatches of hay the full length of the field. Both speed and skill will count for points. Keep your windrows straight boys!"

One after another the horses took their turn. Some were slow, some did well, and some of the drivers slipped up on handling the rake lever and got their windrows crooked. Peter Strong and the bay mare did a perfect job, as before, and at a good smart clip!

Trumper got a little skittish when he started off with the rake, but by the time he got to the hay,

Mark had quieted him with his voice. They went back and forth across the field at a good pace. Mark concentrating desperately on getting his windrows straight. They turned out a good job, and Mark breathed a sigh of relief when it was all over.

"Good boy, Trumper!" Mark said, as he unhitched Trumper from the rake. "You did a good job. Just stay with it now!"

"Time out for lunch." Mr. Hubbard shouted. "The herding will start at one o'clock! There's feed and water for the contestants' horses over by the cattle pen. The horses can be tied there while the boys eat their lunch."

Mark led Trumper over to the pen, watered and fed him, and tied him to the rail. The other horses were already there, munching hungrily at their dinners. Mark and the other boys walked over to the long tables by the road where the food was.

"You and Trumper did mighty well!" Tod said proudly, coming up to Mark at the table. "If you'd ever told me two months ago that Trumper would handle like that, I'd have said you were plumb crazy!"

"Thanks, Dad," Mark said, "but I don't see how he's ever going to beat that bay mare. She's terrific!"

Mark ate one hot dog and a little ice cream and drank a lot of soda pop. He was too nervous to be hungry. He had hoped that by now there'd be some definite hope of victory, but there was none. The judges had given no clue yet as to who was ahead. It was fairly evident that it was between Trumper and Daisy, the bay mare, but Mark had a horrid feeling that the mare had been a little quicker than Trumper. Mark hadn't dared urge Trumper to work faster for fear he'd get excited and mess things up. He wished now that he'd taken a chance on that. Daisy had such quick, easy skill and seemed to be really enjoying the whole thing!

Mark took his last bottle of soda pop with him and went back to see Trumper. He talked to him while he brushed the dry sweat off his sides and put the saddle on his back. He left the bridle till it was time to start, so Trumper could finish his lunch without the bit. Trumper nickered affection- ately as he ate. He seemed to be enjoying the show, too!

Trumper

12

AT ONE O'CLOCK Mr. Hubbard returned to the judges stand and took up his megaphone.

"Saddle up your horses, boys! The herding will start as soon as you're ready. It's only fair to tell you that we've put one ornery cow in the herd. She'll take all the skill you've got to keep her collected. You'll each drive the herd to the end of the field and back, then you'll start out again, and when Mr. Avery yells, 'Now,' you'll stop the herd as quickly as you can and hold them in a tight bunch till he says to go on. Then you'll drive them as far as the wall by the woods, then up to the judges stand, and then back into the pen. If you run them, you're disqualified."

Dick Joel's moth-eaten black was the first to try it. There was no danger of his running them, but the patient horse was completely baffled by the unruly cow who refused to stay rounded up when the herd was stopped.

The other horses did a reasonably good job, but none of them could handle the unruly cow very well. Once she got away altogether and had to be retrieved from the lunch table where she stopped to eat rolls.

Then it was Daisy's turn. She started off with zip, her red-bay coat sleek and shining, and a glint of spirit in her eye. She took the cattle around the field perfectly until she got them to the judges stand. Then the unruly cow broke away and got behind the stand. Peter Strong had a rough time getting her back into the herd. He finally succeeded, and he and the mare got them back into the pen quite neatly.

Trumper had been watching with enthusiasm from the moment the cows were let out of the pen. Herding was his real love, and Mark had to keep holding him back to keep him from joining in on his own.

At last it was Trumper's turn and he swept forward at an easy gallop toward the cattle pen, ears alert, head held high. Again a murmur of admiration went up from the crowd.

"Easy, boy, easy," Mark kept saying. "If you run them you're out. Easy does it!"

Trumper quieted as the cows were let out of the pen. With easy skill he fell in behind them, moving

first to one side then the other, to keep them in a
neat bunch moving straight toward the far end of
the field, where he turned them and started back.
The second time out went as well, then Mr. Avery
shouted "Now!" and Mark and Trumper rounded

the cattle up and brought them to a stop. The unruly cow kept trying to break away, but Trumper
was too quick for her. Mark didn't even have to
guide him. Trumper was watching the cows with
an intent excited expression, moving faster than
they did, outwitting even the unruly one. At the
signal they took the cows to the left, then to the
judges stand.

"For gosh sake, Trumper, be careful now," Mark said softly, keeping a close eye on the cantankerous cow.

But Trumper already had it figured out. He eased up beside her and positively breathed down her neck. She made one or two tries at breaking past him, but no luck. The crowd was breathless with suspense. This was the final test on which the competition hung.

At the judges stand, Mark and Trumper held the herd still for a minute, then turned them toward the pen. The unruly cow made another try as they turned, but Trumper was instantly in front of her, blocking her path. Slowly they moved back across the field toward the pen, Trumper quivering with the intensity of his watchfulness, and Mark holding his breath altogether. Only a few more yards to go, then into the pen. At the gate to the pen, the unruly cow took off! Trumper left the herd and was after her like a shot. Within ten feet he turned her, and forced her back through the gate. A terrific cheer went up from the crowd.

"Will all the boys whose horses have not been disqualified ride up to the judges stand, please," Mr. Hubbard shouted. "The prizes will now be given out."

Mark and Trumper joined the others on the way to the stand. There was mad hope in his heart, but he still wasn't sure. There was a chance that the bay mare had won more points than Trumper with the wagon and rake, and if so the herding job might not count.

When the horses and their riders were lined up before him, Mr. Hubbard introduced the three judges who had helped make the decisions and keep the score of points. Then he put up his hand for silence.

"It gives me great pleasure to announce to you that Mark Sullivan and his horse, Trumper, have won First Prize for the most outstanding performance of the day. It was a mighty close decision as Mark and Peter Strong were tied until the herding. But I think you'll all agree there was no doubt as to who won that! Peter Strong is Second with his bay mare, Daisy, who won last year. And Terry Finch is Third with his white horse Ajax!"

The crowd cheered wildly and Tod came running over to Mark and Trumper.

"You made it, son! You made it!" he shouted excitedly.

Mark was speechless. He couldn't say a word. The bull calf that he'd worked for so long and so determinedly was actually his!

"Oh, Trumper," he finally gasped, "you really, actually did it! You won!"

Trumper nickered happily, dancing a bit, and hoping there was going to be more herding to do.

By that time Carl's and Mark's mother and little

Kathy had joined them, and they all went over to the pen to see the beautiful animal Mark had won. Mark sat there for a moment on Trumper's back, his eyes popping as he looked at the calf close up. It was a well-grown weaner, and it certainly was a beauty! Mark slid out of the saddle, handed Trumper's reins to Tod, and slid through the rails into the pen. The bull calf looked at him with mild, friendly interest, and Mark threw his arms around its neck and hugged it.

The excited crowd had gathered around the pen and everyone was talking at once.

"What a calf!"

"Good work, Mark!"

"That Trumper is some horse. And what a time Mark had training him!"

But Mark didn't even hear them. His whole heart and soul were wrapped up in the Black Angus calf — the beginning of his longed-for beef herd. And Trumper had won it for him!

Peter Strong was bitterly disappointed. Second Prize was a good young ram, but Peter had wanted the bull. He'd won a heifer the year before, but this year the mare had let him down. He'd have to work harder with her before next year.

Third Prize was a young black and white sow and Terry Finch was thrilled with her. It was the first big prize he'd ever won. His father helped load it on their wagon, while Peter Strong led the ram off halfheartedly.

Mr. Hubbard came over and joined the Sullivans at the bull pen. "Hello all of you and congratulations, Mark! You've really won yourself a beauty and you certainly deserve it too. I've been hearing all summer about your troubles with Trumper and the progress you were making. I never thought you'd stand a chance against the Strong's mare! To tell you the truth, I didn't think you'd ever get through the competition without being disqualified. From what I'd heard, Trumper was pretty unpredictable!"

"Oh, he's fine now Mr. Hubbard," Mark said happily. "He just didn't take to farm work, that's all. He likes it all right now. Gee, Mr. Hubbard, thanks for this calf. He sure is a beauty!"

"You earned him fair and square, Mark!" Mr. Hubbard said. "He is a good one, a son of my champion bull. I hope he turns out well for you. I understand you want to start a beef herd. If you win again next year, I'll see that you get a good heifer to go with him. Then you'll be all set to go in business!"

"Gosh, thank you, Mr. Hubbard! That would be wonderful, if Trumper can only win again next time."

"I hope he does, Mark, but I'm afraid Peter Strong

111

was pretty badly disappointed. He won last year, you know, and didn't quite make it this time. That's the way life goes, but I'll bet he'll give you even stiffer competition next year. He won't give up — that's for sure!" Mr. Hubbard stayed and chatted

with Tod and the rest of the family for a bit, then went off to see the other prize winners.

"How are you planning to get the calf home, Mark?" Tod asked. "Carl and I can help you load him on the wagon if you like."

"Oh, no, Dad," Mark exclaimed. "He might fall off and break a leg! Me and Trumper had better herd him home and come back after the milk wagon later!"

"OK, son. We'll follow along in the big wagon in case you have any trouble with him."

Carl hadn't said much. He just stood leaning on the fence looking at the calf, an incredulous look on his face.

"That's some calf, Mark," he said finally. "I never thought you'd really win it with that crazy horse! I figured he'd take one of his moods and go all to pieces when you got him out there on the course. I still don't see how you did it! That's sure some calf."

"I told you Trumper was a good horse!" Mark said, not admitting that he'd been wondering himself how Trumper would behave in a real competition, with all the crowds and excitement.

Mark's mother and little Kathy came to look at the calf. Kathy climbed up on the rail fence and made enthusiastic noises.

"Mark, it's wonderful!" his mother said happily. "Now you really have the beginning of your beef herd."

When most of the crowd had left, Mark climbed up on Trumper's back and signaled Carl to open the gate. The shiny-black weaner looked at the open gate for a minute, then trotted out, glad to be free. Trumper was ready for him and, after a few quick dodges, got him headed down the road for home.

It took quite a bit of herding to get him there as the calf didn't want to leave the farm and the other cattle he had grown up with, but Trumper took no nonsense from him.

Tod and the family were right behind them in the big wagon with the team. When they reached the barn, Tod shouted to Mark to herd the calf inside and they'd fix a place for him for the night.

"Get a rope, Mark," he said when they were all gathered in the barn. "We'll tie him to the ring in the corner till we have time to build something special for him."

The calf had a handsome halter that had come with him, and Mark fastened a hitching rope to it and tied him, then got some clean straw bedding, a pail of water, and some calf feed.

The whole family stood around admiring, hating to leave Mark's wonderful addition to the farm.

"You sure hit the jack pot that time, Mark!" Carl said, still wondering how Mark had ever done it with that Trumper horse.

They finally started milking, and Mark galloped off on Trumper to bring back the milk wagon from the competition grounds. He shouted gaily to Trumper as they tore down the road.

"You did it, boy! You really truly did it!"

Trumper

13

WHEN MARK got home from school the next day, Tod and Carl helped him build a pen for the calf in the corner of the barn. They hauled in stout planks and timbers from the lumber pile, and moved the calf to the other end of the barn while they worked.

"You've got to remember that bull isn't going to stay small like that, Mark," Tod said. "A full grown Black Angus bull is a whale of a big beast, so we'd better make a big pen, and a strong one too."

Tod measured off a space that seemed big enough, and they put stout posts from floor to ceiling to support the heavy plank siding. Mark and Carl nailed the planks in place, while Tod made the gate and hung it with some old iron hinges he found in his tool box. They made the pen four feet high so the bull could see out but couldn't jump over it. When the sides and gate were finished,

Tod built a hayrack in one corner of it, and a feed box beside it.

"Gee, Dad, that looks wonderful!" Mark shouted excitedly. "And it's right handy to the pasture door so I can let him out on good days."

"That's right," Tod said. "These Angus cattle are mighty hardy. He can stay outdoors all winter in the daytime, but you'd better bring him in at night until spring, same as the milk cows. We'd better fence off a special paddock for him near the barn door."

"You know," Carl said, "there's an extra one of those automatic drinking basins on the end cow stanchion that we don't use. I could rig it up in here for you, Mark. Then he'll always have fresh clean water right handy, instead of messing around with a bucket he'll be tipping over all the time.

"Gosh, Carl, that would be wonderful!" Mark yelped excitedly. "It will be just as fancy as Mr. Hubbard's bull pens. Gee, Carl, thanks!"

Carl got some lengths of pipe that were lying by the lumber pile, and after an hour of cutting and fitting the drinking basin was installed and working.

"Jimminy crickets," Mark yipped. "That's super! Thanks, Carl." Mark stood admiring the bull pen in silence for a bit, then went and got straw bedding and hay for the hayrack. When it was ready he led the calf into the pen and took the rope off.

They all stood watching while the calf explored his new quarters, sniffing the fresh golden straw and finally settling down to the hay in the hayrack. He was a friendly fellow from the start. Like all Mr. Hubbard's cattle, he had been well cared for and was used to people.

Mark leaned on the gate of the pen, lost in a daydream of a big herd of Black Angus cattle grazing in a pasture of their own — the handsome bull out in front and numerous sleek, black cows trailing along after him with their tiny, newborn calves beside them. He was so lost in the dream that he forgot to feed and tend the horses when Tod and Carl started milking.

"Look, Mark," Tod said. "How about not neglecting the horses because of that calf. Don't forget that Trumper won him for you!"

"Oh gosh," Mark said, coming out of his daydream with a bang.

But Trumper had no intention of letting Mark forget him. He peered over the side of his stall and nickered impatiently for his supper.

"Coming, Trumper!" Mark said, hastily leaving the calf.

Winter came early that year, with heavy snows and below-zero temperatures. Mark used the pung instead of the wagon for hauling the milk over the white, shiny road to the station. Trumper loved the gay sound of the sleigh bells fastened to its

117

shafts. He loved them so much that when he was standing still he kept shaking himself to keep them ringing. Tod stood watching one morning while Carl loaded the last of the milk cans onto the pung.

"That horse ought to be in the opera instead of on a farm," he said, laughing. "He's a regular old show off. Look at him ring those bells!" Mark and Carl laughed, too, and Trumper looked at them with innocent surprise, wondering what they were laughing at.

Mark didn't like the idea of leaving Trumper in the cold buggy shed while he was at school, so he left him in the warm barn at home, and he and Carl went to school on their skis. They took a short cut across the white, frozen fields and hills, racing each other both ways. Trumper missed the gallops back and forth with Mark, but he was better off in his warm stall.

On Saturdays, Tod and Carl cut stove wood in the wood lot, and Mark hauled it to the house with Trumper and stacked it in the shed. When the shed was filled, they went to the big forest to cut trees for lumber. The huge trees had to be hauled out in winter, when it was easy to skid them on the slippery snow. Later on they'd haul them to the sawmill, but the trick now was to snake them out of the forest while they had the snow to slide them on.

Tod carefully picked the trees to be cut, choosing only the tall, straight ones that would make good planks for building and repairs. He was care-

ful, too, to cut only the crowded ones, leaving more room for the young trees to grow.

"You have to grow wood just the same as any other crop," he said. "If you aren't careful to make room for the young trees to grow in, you just destroy the forest, and in a few years there are no good trees left to cut."

Tod and Carl cut the trees with skilled axe strokes, yelling "Timber!" as each tree fell into a clear space. It was quite a trick to fell a tree just where you wanted it to fall. It meant making the axe cuts exactly right, lower on the side you wanted it to fall toward, and higher on the other side.

Mark's job was to fasten a heavy chain around the end of each felled log and haul it out with the big team. The logs were too heavy for Trumper to pull alone, so Mark had to use Kit and Duke for the job, leaving Trumper in the barn. Trumper didn't like this much, but he had quite a few jobs to do with the pung, and on Sundays he took the family to church in the sleigh, zipping along over the frozen snow with the bells making a merry song behind him.

The bull calf was turned out in his own paddock in the daytime to keep him hardy and strong. He loved the snow and frisked and capered in it, his black hide growing long hair to keep him warm. As the winter grass was buried deep under the snow, Mark had to feed him hay and calf meal three times a day. The calf soon learned that he had to go into the barn to get his dinner, and Mark always found him waiting by the paddock gate at mealtime. He followed Mark without a lead rope, always hungry for his next meal.

The bull's registered name was Black Royal Domino, but Mark felt this was much too long for a half-grown calf and called him Royal for short. It fitted him perfectly. As the weeks went by he grew steadily in size and bulk, and he seemed handsomer every time Mark looked at him. In December, Mr. Hubbard drove over in his sleigh to have a look at him.

"You've been taking good care of him, Mark," he said. "He looks in the pink and he's growing a mile a minute. I think he's going to be a good one!"

Royal grew very attached to Mark and, in spite of his steadily increasing size and strength, he remained gentle and friendly, still following Mark in and out of the barn without a rope. Trumper was often jealous when Mark spent too much time brushing Royal, and he nickered protest from his stall.

"All right, Trumper! I'm going to brush you, too," Mark would say, hurrying over to Trumper's stall. Both Trumper and Royal shone like satin as the result of Mark's loving care and constant brushings.

The Christmas holidays were a welcome break from school and went by altogether too fast. Christmas, as always, was a big day on the farm. Mark had cut a young spruce for a Christmas tree, and he hauled it from the wood lot with a rope tied to Trumper's saddle. Tod had killed the biggest turkey for the occasion, and on Christmas morning the whole house smelled of luscious roasting turkey. Mark's mother had made pies and all the fixings.

They opened their presents first thing in the morning, and Mark's present from the family was a beautiful riding bridle for Trumper. Mark dashed out to the barn to try it on, while the rest of the family finished opening their presents. It had been a good year on the farm and the presents reflected the farm's prosperity. Tod gave his wife a washing machine, something she'd never had before. There'd be no more hand scrubbing of dirty farm clothes now! Tod got a sheepskin-lined jacket, and Carl got a whole stack of radio parts for building his set. Kathy got a new sled.

After the presents, they all stuffed on turkey and pie until they nearly burst. Mark and Carl went skiing with the boys at the next farm after dinner. It was a gay and festive day and was over all too soon.

The rest of the winter, with its short, bright days and long nights went by slowly, the snow drifting deeper and deeper as the months went on. The barn was dark and warm, coming into it out of the shining frozen snow, and Mark spent a great deal of time there after school. Often the snow was too deep for outside chores, and Tod and the boys puttered with inside jobs that needed doing.

Finally spring came, arriving with a sudden warm wind in March that melted patches in the snow. Brown mud began to show between the

drifts, and big puddles formed in the ruts along the lane. Thin sheets of ice still covered them at night, but in the day they made a lovely sploshing sound as the horses walked through them.

In another two weeks the green began to show, before the last of the snow was gone. The April sun shone down steadily, and the creek was a bubbling torrent fed by the fast-melting snow. By mid-April the cows were turned out to graze the early spring grass, and Royal munched happily at the new green shoots in his paddock. He was fatter and sleeker than ever.

The ground was still too wet for plowing and planting, but there was plenty to do getting ready for the busiest time of year ahead. Carl checked over all the farm equipment, oiling and repairing it, while Mark and his father mended fences dragged down by the heavy snow.

In May, Tod settled down to plowing with the big team. It was hard work and both he and the team were hot and tired by the end of the day. It was a job that had to be done alone, driving Kit and Duke back and forth across the big fields, Tod walking behind the plow and guiding it in the furrow. The planting was easier on Tod and the horses both. The planter was lighter than the plow, and Tod could ride on the seat.

As soon as the snow was gone, Mark began practicing with Trumper for the next 4-H Club competition. Now that he had the bull, he was more than ever determined to win the heifer. Then he'd have the real beginning of a herd! He worked Trumper hard with the milk wagon, and on Sundays he set up a course with sticks and practiced Trumper in backing long distances without touching them.

They worked at the herding, too, but this was never work for Trumper because he loved it. To him it was a game, and his favorite one at that!

Trumper

14

WHEN SCHOOL let out in June they started haying. The weather was perfect for it, day after day of bright sunshine, and the hay dried quickly. Mark and Trumper raked it with real enthusiasm this year, and Mark was determined to teach Trumper to do a fast and perfect job of it. The windrows were beautifully straight after two weeks of work on it, and by the time haying was finished they had added speed to skill.

The loft of the barn was filled to bursting and it looked like another good crop year for the farm. But after haying the sun went on shining. Day after day it rose into the same cloudless sky, and night after night it sank like a red, fiery ball in the west, promising more hot, dry weather ahead.

At first it seemed ideal weather for getting the outside jobs done, and Tod and the boys tackled them happily enough, the boys taking time out for swimming in the creek to cool off. But as the dry weather went on week after week, the oats and corn stopped growing and began to turn yellow in the fields. Tod was worried.

"Only two rains since the first of June," he said. "If this keeps on we'll lose most of the oats and corn!"

It did keep on. Every morning Tod searched the sky for clouds, but there were none. As the sun rode up into the clear blueness of the sky, a haze of heat rose off the land giving a misty look to the hills. The nights were hot and dry, too, with almost no dew to moisten the leaves of the crops. The grass was already brown, and when a breeze stirred the ten acres of corn near the farmhouse, its dry leaves rustled together, making a whispering in the night.

The corn was only half its normal height, and the oat stems were so brittle that they broke in every breeze, leaving flat areas where they should have stood straight and strong. It was essential to have enough corn in the silo to feed the twenty milk cows through the long winter, and the horses must have oats. There was good soil on the Sullivan farm and Tod was a skillful farmer. Each year he planted a surplus of oats and corn in order to sell the extra, adding to the cash income of the farm.

"There'll be no extra to sell this year," Tod said, shaking his head. "We'll be lucky if we get enough to feed the stock."

Relentlessly the sun went on beating down on the dry earth, drawing the moisture out from deep

below the surface. July slipped by, and August came in hotter than ever. By early August it was too late for rain to help. The crops were dry and brown. They'd do no more growing now.

Tod looked sadly at the scrubby fields, deep lines of worry in his face. "It's no use leaving the oats and corn standing there any longer," he said. "It'll all be flat on the ground if we do. A rain now would just break off every brittle stalk and wreck the last of it. We'd better harvest what there is right away!"

The next morning he hitched Kit and Duke to the harvester and started on the oats. Mark hitched Trumper to the milk wagon and followed the harvester, while Carl forked the scanty oats aboard. The milk wagon didn't hold much at a time, but the crop was so scanty it hardly seemed worthwhile to use the big wagon. A sudden rain would have destroyed what was left, so it seemed best for Tod to keep the big team steadily at work on the harvester.

Trumper worked well in spite of the scorching heat that soaked his sides with sweat. In two days the whole of the miserable little crop was cut and stacked by the loft door, ready for the threshing machine. Tod had already sent a hurry call for Big Joe and his ancient steam engine, and they arrived as Mark and Trumper hauled the last load to the barn.

It didn't take long to thresh the scant crop that year. They stopped at noon for lunch, and by three in the afternoon the job was finished. Only one feed bin was filled. Tod and Big Joe looked at it sadly.

"It's the same all over this part of the country," Big Joe said. "No rain, no oats!"

Tod nodded his head gloomily. "Don't know what we're going to feed the horses this winter," he said. "There isn't enough there to feed them two months on scant rations. They'll have to live on hay, and that won't keep them going till the next crop is ready. And if the corn is as bad as this, we'll have to save most of the hay for the cows! There'll be no money to buy feed this year."

The corn was even worse than the oats. The stalks that should have been green and juicy to make good ensilage, were dry and shrunken, and the ears of corn had hardly formed at all. When the harvesting was finished, the silo was less than a quarter full.

"There'll be no crop money this year," Tod told his wife. "We'll have to save every penny to buy at least a little cow feed. The horses can manage on hay when they aren't working too hard, but cows just won't give milk without corn. And the chickens won't lay without grain either. We're in for a mighty tough year, Katherine!"

Tod's wife tried to look hopeful and cheer him up, but she knew just how desperate the situation was. Nothing to do but take one day at a time and hope and pray they'd be able to get through somehow.

Mark had turned Royal out in the meadow by the creek, hoping he'd find enough second-growth grass to keep him going. He'd been fed grain three times a day to supplement the brown grass, and he was in beautiful condition, despite the drought. He was nearly full grown now, and a really handsome beast. Mark rode out to the field three times a day on Trumper with a measure of grain. While Royal ate, Mark brushed him to keep his black hide sleek and shining.

"No grain for you or Trumper either this winter," Mark said sadly, stroking Royal's shining neck. "I just hope Dad will let me feed you grain till the County Fair comes so I can show you in good shape. It's only ten days off now!"

That night Mark pled with his father for enough grain to feed Royal till the Fair. "He can eat hay after that, Dad!" Mark said. "It won't hurt him then. He's got most of his growth now. But if I take him off grain before the Fair, he won't stand a chance of winning a prize."

"I don't know what good a prize will do us, Mark," Tod said. "You can't eat ribbons, not even a blue one! But if you want to feed him grain the next ten days, you'll just have to take Trumper off it. He isn't working very hard now and he'll be all right on hay, and you're not showing him."

The next morning when Mark gave Kit and Duke their oats, Trumper nickered impatiently for his. "I'm sorry, Trumper," Mark said. "I've got to give yours to Royal, just for ten days so he'll look right for the Fair! Then I guess you'll all be eating hay."

Trumper had no idea what Mark was talking about, and he went on nickering impatiently for his oats. Mark didn't have the heart to ride Trumper out to the fields where he'd have to watch Royal eating his grain, so he walked, carrying the full measure in his hand. He heard Trumper still nickering hungrily in the barn.

Labor Day weekend was cooler, but the sun still beat down on the drought-parched earth. The fields were brown and stubbly instead of green, and the leaves were already falling from the trees.

The bull judging was to be on Monday afternoon. Monday morning, when Mark and Trumper got back from taking the milk to the station Mark tied Royal to the back of the wagon with a short lead rope. Tod climbed aboard with Mark and they set off slowly for the Fair, Royal following amiably behind the wagon, his hide glistening from Mark's many brushings.

There was no feeling of happy festivity about going to the Fair this year, and Tod only went because Mark was so anxious to show his beloved bull. They drove along in silence most of the way, Mark holding Trumper down to a walk to keep from overheating the bull.

The County Fair was a busy place, as always, but there were fewer people this year and fewer entries because of the drought. The whole countryside was depressed and anxious over the hungry winter that lay ahead, especially the dairy farmers who needed corn to keep their cows milking!

Mark tied Trumper to a hitching rail near the bull shed and untied Royal from the wagon.

"Well, Mark," Tod said, trying to sound cheerful, "I surely hope you win something on that bull of yours. He certainly is a beauty and, even if we can't eat ribbons, it would be cheering to win one! We could stand some cheering!"

"If he does win a prize, Dad, it will help my beef herd when I get it rolling!" Mark said. "The calves will bring a much better price with a prize bull for their father!"

They led Royal over to the shed and into the stall reserved for him. Most of the bulls were already there, and a handsome bunch they were. There were Holsteins and Guernseys and Herefords, and ten Black Angus. Tod wanted to have a look at the Holsteins, but Mark headed straight for the Black Angus, anxious to see what kind of competition there was. He was discouraged when he saw. All but two of the bulls were certainly outstanding, and Mark couldn't decide whether they were better than Royal or not.

Tod came over and joined him. "Boy! You've certainly got some stiff competition there," he said. "What a bunch of beauties!"

They went back to Royal's stall and watered and fed him. They got sandwiches and soda pop for themselves, then returned to the stall to give Royal a final polishing after his dusty journey.

At two o'clock the judging of the Black Angus bulls was announced over the loud speaker. All the dairy bulls had been judged that morning. Mark led Royal out to the ring and Tod went to find a seat to watch the judging. Royal kept looking around nervously at the crowd and the other bulls, but he kept quietly beside Mark, trusting his master.

The eleven Black Angus bulls paraded around

the ring twice, the judges watching their action as they walked. Then they were ordered into the center of the ring, where they were lined up for individual judging. The judges started at the other end of the line from Mark and Royal and went over each bull from end to end. They looked at them from every angle, felt them all over for defects of bone or muscle, and felt the smoothness of their coats. It took a long time, and Mark was growing weary with suspense and standing in the hot sun. Royal finally closed his eyes and dozed.

Trumper

15

AFTER NEARLY AN HOUR the judges got to Mark and
Royal. Royal woke up with a start and held his head
handsomely alert, snorting a little as the strangers
came close and felt him over. Mark held his breath.
The judges took a long time over Royal. They con-
sulted their score pads, and even went back to look
at two other bulls. Then they came back to Royal
and, with a smile at Mark, they pinned the Blue
Ribbon on Royal's halter!

Mark could hardly believe it. Royal had won
First Prize! In a minute Tod was out of his seat
and in the ring beside Mark. "Good work!" he
shouted excitedly. "First Prize! You certainly can't
do any better than that. Let's get home and tell the
family. I bet they won't believe it till they see the
ribbon!"

Mark was too excited to speak. He just sputtered happily as they started to lead Royal to the wagon. Suddenly a well-dressed man came over to them and spoke to Tod.

"That's quite a bull you have there, sir!"

"He's not mine," Tod said. "He belongs to my son here. He won him a year ago in a 4-H Club competition with his horse. He raised him from a weaner all himself."

"Well you surely won something worthwhile that time," the man said. "I'm Mr. Blake of the Pine Tree Black Angus Farm, and I'd be mighty interested in buying that bull from you, son."

"Oh he's not for sale!" Mark said quickly. "I'm going to start a beef herd myself if I win the heifer this year! I wouldn't part with Royal for anything!"

"Would you part with him for two thousand dollars?" Mr. Blake asked. "I need a new blood line in my herd, and I understand this is a son of Mr. Hubbard's champion bull. Is that right?"

"That's right," Mark gasped, his eyes as big as saucers. He didn't know anything was worth two thousand dollars!

"Gee, Mark!" Tod exclaimed. "Two thousand would buy feed for the stock all winter and save the farm!"

Mark's face turned suddenly white and tense.

"You wouldn't sell Royal, would you, Dad!" he

said incredulously. "He's the beginning of my beef herd!"

"He's not mine to sell, Mark," Tod said. "He's yours. It would save the farm, but I know how much you think of that bull, and you won him fair

and square your own self. It's your decision to make, Mark."

Mark's face suddenly twisted as if he were going to cry right then and there. He bit his lips, struggling to hold back the tears. He wished from the bottom of his heart that he hadn't brought Royal to the Fair and that he hadn't won First Prize. He stood there in an agony of indecision. He knew how desperate the situation was at the farm, but he also knew that without a bull he'd have no herd, even if he won the heifer this year. There'd be no third chance at the 4-H Club to win another bull. You could only win the competition twice. That was the ruling.

Mr. Blake looked at Mark's stricken face. "I guess we'd better call the whole thing off, son. You'd better keep your bull for your own herd. I surely would like to have him, but I didn't realize how much he meant to you!"

Mark looked at Tod. Tod's face had lost its sudden look of hope and settled back into the grim look of worry it had had ever since the drought wrecked the crops. Mark took a deep breath, trying to steady his voice and choke back the sobs that were making it hard to swallow.

"I guess I'd better sell him, Mr. Blake," Mark said in a choked voice. "There won't even be enough feed for Trumper if I don't, and Dad said we'd be lucky if we didn't lose the farm altogether because of the drought!"

Mr. Blake was silent. He looked at Tod, but Tod said nothing, leaving the decision entirely up to Mark.

"I'll tell you what I'll do, son," Mr. Blake said finally. "I have a young weaner bull calf in the show here. He only won Third Prize, but he's young yet and he's good stock. He's a son of my champion. I'll give you seventeen hundred dollars for your bull, and the weaner besides. That will give you two blood lines for your herd if you win Mr. Hubbard's heifer this year."

Mark looked at Tod again. "Seventeen hundred would certainly help the farm!" Tod said. "But it's still up to you to decide, Mark."

"Let's go look at the weaner," Mr. Blake suggested. "My man can hold Royal while we go." Reluctantly Mark gave Royal's lead rope to the farm hand who had joined them, and they went into the calf shed. Mr. Blake's weaner was in a stall at the far end eating hay, a yellow ribbon fastened to his halter. Mark looked at him in silence for a long time, his heart still torn to bits at the thought of parting with his beloved Royal. The calf was handsome but he was at the awkward age and didn't look like much compared to the magnificent full-grown bull! Maybe Royal had looked like that, too, when he was that age, but Mark could only think of him as he looked now.

Mark went into the stall and held out his hand to the calf. The calf licked it, looking at Mark with big round eyes. "I guess I'd better take him," Mark said, his voice still trembling. "We've just got to save the farm somehow."

"It's mighty good of you to offer to include the calf at such a bargain price, Mr. Blake," Tod said. "He's worth a lot more than that I know!"

"Yes he is," Mr. Blake said. "But I want Mark's bull very badly, and I hate to take away the boy's chance of having a herd of his own. I'd do a good deal to own that Royal bull!"

Mark stroked the weaner's neck in silence, still overcome at the thought of losing Royal.

"Is it a deal, Mark?" Mr. Blake asked.

"I guess so," Mark said sadly.

"Good boy!" Mr. Blake said heartily. He untied the calf's rope and handed it to Mark. "Here's the calf, and I'll make you a check for Royal right now! Shall I make it out to you or your Dad?"

"You'd better give it to Dad," Mark said. "He'll be the one to buy the feed with it."

Mr. Blake wrote the check and handed it to Tod.

Tod hesitated over taking it and turned to Mark.

"Are you sure this is the way you want it, Mark?" he asked.

"Yes, Dad," Mark answered as firmly as he could with his voice still shaking. "We've just got to save the farm, and at least Trumper will have something to eat now."

"You're doing a fine thing," Tod said softly, knowing how terribly torn Mark was.

Mark led the calf out of its stall and they went outside to where Royal was standing. Suddenly Mark threw his arms around Royal's neck, the hot tears coming in spite of his struggle to hold them back.

"You're going away, Royal," Mark sobbed. "You've got to save the farm! There isn't any other way!"

Tod and Mr. Blake watched in silence, unable to speak themselves.

"You will be good to him, won't you, Mr. Blake?" Mark asked, turning to Royal's new owner. "He's used to a lot of petting and brushing, you know."

"He'll be treated like the royal king he is, Mark," Mr. Blake said. "He'll have the best of feed, and a big pasture to graze in, and a warm barn in winter. And you can come and see him anytime you want to make the trip!"

"I'll come!" Mark said. "I can ride there on Trumper sometime."

"Good boy. I'll show you my herd and the whole farm. Any time I can be of help to you with your herd, let me know. And I surely hope you win the heifer so you'll really be in business! Goodbye now, and good luck."

Mr. Blake shook hands with them both, and he and the farm hand led Royal away. Mark watched them go, biting his lips to keep from crying again. Royal looked back twice, and once he stopped and tried to turn back to Mark. Then they went out of sight behind the bull shed.

Tod stood looking at the check. "One thousand, seven hundred dollars!" he said. "That will feed the stock and pay the mortgage all winter, Mark! We'll still have to be mighty careful with the feed to make it last, but this should see us through. I don't know how to thank you for what you just did!"

"It's all right, Dad," Mark said, feeling more like a man than a boy. He and Trumper had saved the farm, Trumper by winning Royal in the competition, and Mark by raising and selling him. Through the pain of parting there came a little thread of happiness and hope. The farm would come through now, and he still had the beginning of a beef herd! It wasn't Royal, but it was a bull, and who could tell what good feeding and care would do for the new weaner calf. Mark looked at it with new interest, and the calf looked back with curi-

143

osity and gentleness in its big, round eyes.

"Let's take him home, Dad, and show him to the family, and tell them about Royal winning First Prize and the farm being saved!"

"That we'll do," Tod said, looking as if an immense and painful load had been lifted from his shoulders.

Trumper nickered from the hitching rail when he saw them coming. He looked curiously at the calf and looked around for Royal.

"He's sold," Mark said, "and the farm is saved and now you'll be able to eat all winter, Trumper!"

They tied the calf to the back of the wagon and Mark headed Trumper for home. They didn't say much on the long drive. They were both lost in thought, Tod dreaming happily of the feed he could buy to keep the cows milking and the horses working, and Mark dreaming of his herd and hoping desperately that the new calf would grow as handsome as Royal had been. The main thing now was to win the heifer!

They got to the farmhouse at supper time. Carl had done the milking and fed the horses alone. He and his mother and little Kathy came out on the porch when they saw them coming.

"Where's Royal?" Carl and his mother asked in one breath.

"He won First Prize, Mom, and I sold him to save the farm!" Mark shouted. "Mr. Blake bought him, and he gave me this calf at a bargain to close the deal!"

Mark's mother looked at his tear-stained face and knew just what it had meant to part with Royal.

"Oh, Mark, that's wonderful!" she said. "What a beautiful calf! And he's won a ribbon, too!"

Tod handed the check to his wife. She looked at it, then looked again, hardly believing what it said.

"Seventeen hundred!" she exclaimed. "Why, that will see us through the winter and save the farm! I had no idea Royal was worth all that. Oh, Tod, how wonderful."

"It was Mark that did it!" Tod said. "I left the decision up to him, entirely. We have Mark and Trumper to thank for saving the farm. I didn't do any of it at all."

Mark grinned for the first time since Royal was sold. There was a good feeling growing inside where all the pain had been.

Trumper

16

Two WEEKS after the Fair, Mark woke up in the night to the sound of heavy rain beating on the roof like a chorus of drums. The drought was broken at last! Water gurgled noisily in the down spouts, spilling over and falling in pools on the ground below. It was a good sound after the long dryness, and Mark lay in bed listening. He could tell by the sound of it that it was a real drencher, the kind of long, steady rain that soaks to the roots and restores life to the soil.

Mark wondered if the big maple by the gate would come back to life now. It had looked dead so long, its leaves lying brown and shriveled on the ground around it instead of turning crimson and gold.

Carl was still asleep in his bunk across the attic bedroom and it was too dark to see the tin alarm clock on the bureau. Mark wondered drowsily what time it was. A cold wind was flapping the window curtains, and he snuggled deeper under his blankets, listening dreamily to the comforting sound of the rain. Why had it come so late, he wondered, too late to save the crops, too late to save Royal from being sold. If only the drought hadn't happened he could have kept Royal! There would have been plenty of feed as usual and no need to sell him to save the farm. But there was no way to make the drought unhappen or to bring Royal back now.

Mark tossed and turned uneasily, wondering how the new bull would turn out, and whether he would win the heifer in the competition this year and really have a herd at last. Finally he fell asleep again and dreamed his favorite dream of a huge field filled with Black Angus cattle, and he and Trumper herding them skillfully about. The rain went on steadily outside, gathering in pools, running in little streams over the heat-baked soil, seeking out every crack and crevice to soak down to the thirsty roots below.

When Mark woke up again it was morning and still raining hard. A heavy, gray sky stood outside the window, and he could see the bare maple branches swaying blackly against it in the wind. He jumped out of bed and shouted to Carl to wake up. Carl grunted sleepily and turned over.

"Wake up!" Mark shouted. "It's raining! A real drencher!"

"Ugh," Carl muttered. "What does it have to do that for on a school day! We'll get soaked!"

"But the drought's broken!" Mark yelped excitedly.

"Too late to help anything," Carl grumbled sleepily.

Mark jumped into his clothes and charged down the stairs shouting, "It's raining! It's raining!"

Tod looked up from his coffee with a grin. "It's raining all right," he said. "Too bad we didn't get this two months ago. It would have saved the crops."

Carl came sleepily down to the kitchen to get his breakfast, still grumbling about the rain coming too late to do any good. Mark finished eating and got his heavy rain slicker and hat out of the closet. They were stiff from long lack of use.

Mark got to the barn first, and Trumper nickered his usual welcome. Mark stopped to pat him, then dashed over to look at the new bull calf. Every morning Mark looked at him to see if he'd grown any handsomer or looked more like Royal. The calf gave a friendly little moo and came over to Mark for food and petting. Mark scratched him behind the ears, looking him over carefully. It did seem as if he were growing handsomer.

Mark fed the horses and the calf and harnessed

148

Trumper to take the milk to the station, while Tod and Carl did the milking.

"We'd better leave the cows in the barn pasture," Tod said. "Easier to get them in tonight in the rain. Why don't you drive straight to school in the wagon, Mark, after you leave the milk at the station? You could take Carl with you."

Trumper laid back his ears when Carl climbed onto the front seat of the wagon. "I'd rather walk in the rain than drive with that crazy horse!" Carl said, eying distrustfully Trumper's explosive look.

"It's all right, Trumper," Mark said. "I'm going to do the driving." Trumper turned his head and watched Mark climb onto the seat and take up the reins, then put his ears forward where they belonged and started off at his usual steady trot. Tod stood in the barn door, laughing. "That horse is crazy, all right!" he said to himself. "Still won't let anybody but Mark drive him!"

When the boys got home from school that day, there was a big envelope addressed to Mark in the letter box. It was from Mr. Blake, and the new calf's pedigree and registration papers were in it, along with a short note from Mr. Blake.

> Dear Mark,
>
> Here are the papers for your new bull, and just a line to tell you that Royal is fine and seems happy in his new home. He surely is a beauty and I hope your new bull will turn

149

out just as well. He certainly should with the pedigree he has.

Your friend,

Tom Blake

"Yippee," Mark shouted. "Royal is fine! And here are the papers for the new calf. Gee, Dad, look!"

It was an impressive document. At the top it gave the bull's name and registration number. "Scottish Chief III," Mark read. "Gee, what a wonderful name! I'll call him Chief for short! And look, Dad, his father was Champion Scottish Chief II! He really is the son of a champion, just like Royal!"

Tod and Carl both looked at the papers. "Whew!" Tod exclaimed. "He certainly ought to go places with a pedigree like that! It's every bit as good as Royal's."

Mark dashed off to the barn in the rain to tell the calf his name and look him over again.

It rained for two weeks, the same steady downpour, day and night, drenching the tree roots and the long-parched soil and filling the wells. Mark really did love the rain. He loved the sound and the smell of it, and the fresh damp wind after the long scorching heat. And he loved it for soaking the thirsty soil and saving the trees before winter came. But he was worried because it kept him from practicing with Trumper for the competition!

The rain finally stopped the first week in October. There were only five days left before the

competition, and Mark spent the weekend and every free minute practicing with the hayrake and milk wagon.

"If we don't win the heifer I still won't have a herd, Trumper," he said. "You've just got to do better than ever! Dick Joel has a new black horse they say is a corker. And Pete Strong will be driving that Daisy mare again, and you know she darn near beat you last year. We've got to do a terrific job to win this time!" Trumper nickered and tossed his head. He didn't know what Mark was talking about, but he was more than willing to do anything Mark wanted him to.

The day of the competition was cloudy and cold, but it didn't rain, and a good crowd turned out for it as usual. The trees were bare this year from the drought, but new shoots of green grass were struggling up after the long rain. It had been hard to find enough second-growth hay to cut for the raking competition, and what there was lay thin and brittle in the field. It wouldn't be easy to rake that short, scrubby stuff into neat windrows!

Mark looked at the heifer in the prize pen as he drove past. She looked awfully big for a calf and she surely was a beauty! He wondered if she really was the prize this year, or if there was a calf somewhere in another pen. He drove over and joined the competitors, giving a quick, anxious look at the other horses. Instantly his eye fell on Dick Joel's new black at the head of the line. He gave a gasp of anxiety and his heart sank.

The black stood tall and handsome, his ears pricked forward with spirit. His eyes had a look of keen intelligence that made Mark's heart sink lower still, until it felt as if it were in the middle of his stomach.

"Gosh, Trumper!" he said softly. "How can we ever beat that one and the bay mare, too. Some difference from the old moth-eaten horse he drove last year!" Daisy, the bay mare, looked in better

shape than ever, and Pete Strong had a look of determination in his eye that boded no good!

"We'll just have to do the very best we can, Trumper!" Mark said grimly. "That's all we can do! And for gosh sakes take it easy and don't get excited. Fast and steady is our only chance, but don't get excited and mess things up."

All but the black were the same horses that had competed last year. Mark was at the end of the line this time, Number Nine. He lived farther from the field than the others, and they'd all got there before him, but Mark was glad to be last. It meant that he could watch all the others first and try to concentrate on doing better in whatever they slipped up on. But it did mean long waiting and suspense, too!

The competition started with the new black turning out an absolutely perfect performance with the milk wagon. He had zip, style, and speed, and he backed fast and skillfully between the flags. Mark groaned softly to himself.

Only one horse was disqualified this year for knocking down a flag. They all seemed to be doing better as the result of careful practicing this time. The crowd cheered several of the performances, but the black and the bay mare were top favorites till Mark drove out into the field with Trumper. The crowd remembered last year's winner and cheered as soon as he drove out. Trumper skittered a little at the sudden noise, but steadied down as Mark talked softly and pleadingly to him. He went through the course perfectly and faster than last year. At the end of the milk wagon competition, it looked as if the three top horses were exactly even.

Hayraking was next, and the eight remaining horses and drivers tried their luck at it. It was a miserable job, trying to rake the short, scrubby hay. The windrows had to be farther apart to get enough hay in them, and this threw some of the drivers off in handling the rake lever. Some of the windrows were badly crooked as a result. But, at the end of the raking, it still looked as if the three top horses were an even tie! There had never been such excitement at the competition before.

Mark, Pete Strong, and Dick Joel, walked over to the lunch tables together, giving each other uneasy glances and not saying much. None of them ate much, and even the crowd hurried with lunch, anxious to get back to the next event, the cattle herding. Everything depended on that now!

Trumper

17

AFTER LUNCH, the boys saddled their horses and the crowd hurried back to the field, everyone trying to get in front of everybody else to get a better view of the doings.

The unruly cow was still in the herd and, as Mr. Hubbard pointed out laughingly, she was a year older, wiser, and more cussed than she'd been last time. "No one will be disqualified for running her," he added, "because she'll run anyway! She always does. Just don't run the others."

He wished the boys luck, and the herding competition began. Dick Joel's new black was first, and he swung out into the field at an easy gallop. A murmur of applause went up from the crowd as Dick turned the big horse easily and drew him to a stop by the gate of the cattle pen. The gate was opened and the cattle poured out with the unruly cow in the lead, looking for trouble.

Dick and the black took them successfully to the end of the field at a walk, but on the way back the unruly cow kept trying to break out of the herd, first on one side and then on the other. The black was too quick for her and managed to keep her in line, but on the next trip out she got away and charged for the woods, the black in hot pursuit!

When she reached the low stone wall, the cow scrambled over it and disappeared into the woods. Dick urged his horse over the wall and went after her, and in a few minutes they came back over the wall and tore across the field toward the rest of the herd. The crowd cheered, but the black horse lost his head in the excitement of the chase and Dick couldn't slow him fast enough. He charged into the middle of the herd and they scattered at a dead run.

"Sorry!" Mr. Hubbard shouted from the judging stand. "We'll have to disqualify you, Dick, for running the herd. It's too bad, because you've put in a perfect performance in everything else. Better luck next year!"

Dick pulled the black over to the side lines, bitter disappointment in his face. A mounted farm hand went after the scattered herd and finally got them back in the pen.

The next four horses didn't get to first base. The

unruly cow was in a real mood today, and what followed was more like a rodeo than a herding competition. Cows were all over the place as the baffled horses tried to outwit the unruly one. Three horses were disqualified for running the herd, and the fourth gave up after half an hour, with cows scattered from end to end of the field.

Pete Strong and his bay mare were next, and Mark watched with his heart in his mouth. They took the cows back and forth across the field with better skill than last year, outwitting the unruly cow at every turn. They got them safely up to the judges stand at last, held them, then turned them back to the pen, the last lap of the job. Halfway to the pen the unruly beast slipped across in front of the herd and charged away before Pete and the mare could get around the remaining cows.

They left the herd where it was and tore across the field in hot pursuit. It took ten minutes of fast riding to round her up. The others had scattered all over the field in the meantime, and it took another ten minutes to collect them and get them into the pen. Time was important, but at least he'd made it and he won an enthusiastic cheer from the crowd.

Terry Finch was next on his clever, white horse, but the unruly cow had them licked from the start. He struggled with it till Mr. Hubbard shouted that the time was up, and he returned to the side lines looking sad. The farm hand had to put the herd back in the pen, and it took him half an hour to do it!

It was late afternoon before Trumper's turn came, and Mark hoped desperately that the fading daylight would last. Trumper pranced out into the field full of impatience from the long wait.

"Easy, Trumper. Easy!" Mark said softly.

"You'll wreck everything if you go at it like that!"

Trumper quieted a little, but he was still dancing as he waited by the gate for the cattle to come out. The unruly one came out first, as usual, gave a snort at Trumper, and walked off down the field as if she had no mean intentions at all. Neither Trumper nor Mark was fooled by her and they watched her every second. They went across the field and back with no major trouble, then off toward the woods, where the unruly beast decided to try that trick again. She was three feet from the low wall when Trumper tore in front of her and stopped. She turned on a dime and charged back to the herd.

Mark remembered what had happened to Dick and the black. He hauled on Trumper's reins, holding him back from his impulsive charge after the cow. The cow rushed into the herd, but instead of scattering they gave her a bored look and went on standing there. If a horse had rushed them it would have been different! Mark held Trumper at a little distance till the commotion settled down, then rode slowly out and herded them to the judges stand. Trumper held them still for a minute, then turned them back toward the pen.

"Easy, Trumper!" Mark kept saying. "For gosh sake watch them now, and don't rush them!"

Trumper followed them, watching the uncooperative one every minute. Halfway to the pen, she took off, just as she had with Pete Strong. Trumper

160

tried to follow, but Mark held him back. "Put the others in the pen first, Trumper! Then we'll go after her! It will be quicker that way!"

He guided Trumper after the herd and put them through the gate at a fast walk. Before the last one was quite in, Mark wheeled Trumper around and they tore across the field at a dead gallop. The unruly cow had slowed down when she found no one was following her, and she was walking casually toward the wall by the woods.

Mark swung Trumper in a wide curve around her, to keep from startling her into a mad run for the wall. She saw their scheme just before they got to her and tried to make a getaway, but Trumper was too fast for her and she wheeled around, heading for the far end of the field. Trumper outran her before she got to the end of it and turned her again. He was really miffed with that cow now, and he reached out and gave her a sharp nip on the rump as he turned her. The crowd howled with laughter!

They tore across the field toward the pen, Trumper holding her in a straight line and nipping her rump every time she tried to break out of it. A wild cheer mixed with laughter went up as she shot into the pen as if the devil were after her. She plowed into the middle of the herd for protection from Trumper, and the farm hand shut the gate. Trumper stood still, panting, and Mark looked anxiously toward the judges stand. He saw Mr. Hubbard step forward to announce the winner.

"I guess there's no doubt about who won that one!" he laughed. "Mark Sullivan and his horse, Trumper, have won First Prize for the second and last time. With them out of the competition next year, the rest of you boys may stand a chance! Ride up boys, as I call your names. Mark Sullivan First, Peter Strong and Daisy Second, and I guess we'll give Third to Terry Finch as nobody else got anywhere near it. Terry was doing all right, he just ran out of time! If he'd had another two days to do it in, he'd have had it made, and his score was good in the other events."

Mark and Trumper were still panting from their wild pursuit of the unruly cow.

"Oh gosh! Thank you, Mr. Hubbard!" Mark panted, and he urged Trumper over to the prize pen to see the heifer.

"Gee," Mark exclaimed. "*She* can't be the one! She's no calf! She's at least a whole year old."

"That's right," Mr. Hubbard said, coming up beside him. "Fourteen months to be exact. And she's expecting a calf sired by my champion! It should be born in the early spring, Mark."

"But — but — gosh, Mr. Hubbard!" Mark sputtered. "That's like winning two Black Angus instead of one!"

"I'll tell you why I did it Mark," Mr. Hubbard

said. "Mr. Blake told me about your selling Royal to him to save your father's farm, and how badly you felt about it. It was a mighty fine thing to do! I figured there was a good chance of your winning again this year, so I decided to fix it so you'd have a going herd if you did win!"

Tod had come up behind them and heard the conversation. "Well if that isn't the kindest thing I ever heard of!" he exclaimed.

"You know, Tod," Mr. Hubbard said, "I like the way Mark takes responsibility about things. He showed that in his determination to teach Trumper to work, and when he sold Royal to save the farm. It's the kind of spirit I like to see!"

Mark was leaning on the fence looking at the heifer.

"Gee, what a beauty," he kept saying. "And she's going to have a calf! Gosh, Mr. Hubbard, THANKS!"

"Her name is Royal Josephine," Mr. Hubbard said, patting Mark on the back.

"That's beautiful," Mark said. "And it has a Royal in it. Is she related to Royal, Mr. Hubbard?"

"She's his young sister," Mr. Hubbard said.

"Gosh! How wonderful!" Mark yelped. "I guess I'll call her Josie, though, for short."

Finally the crowd thinned out and the Sullivans gathered around Mark, admiring the heifer.

"I think I'll walk home," Mark said. "I can lead

Trumper and the heifer. I wouldn't want her to get tired or frightened or anything if she's going to have a calf!"

He hurried off with Trumper, unsaddled him, hitched him to the wagon, and came back to get the heifer. He took Trumper's bridle in one hand and the heifer's lead rope in the other, and they started slowly up the road, the farm wagon with the family following behind.

"Gosh, Trumper," Mark said lovingly. "Just look what you won now!"

After winning Josie, Mark started disappearing whenever he had time off. One Saturday he saddled Trumper and led him to the storeroom at the end of the wagon shed. He hauled out a bulky something, got hammer and nails, and climbed on Trumper's back with the lot. He rode past the farmhouse to the big maple by the gate. The family had just gathered for dinner when they saw Mark ride by, carrying something big.

"Now what's that boy up to just at meal time!" Tod said.

They went out to look. Mark was standing on Trumper's back, nailing a beautifully carved and painted sign to the tree. The Sullivans went out in the road to see it better.

At the top of the sign was a handsomely carved Black Angus bull, and below it in neat lettering it said:

MARK SULLIVAN
BLACK ANGUS CATTLE
CHAMPION STOCK

"Well, I'll be!" Tod said.

Mark drove the last nail in and slid down off Trumper's back.

"There it is, Trumper!" Mark said. "The beef herd is really begun, and you won it for me!"

Trumper nickered happily and tossed his head.